The Eleventh Summer

CARLO GÉBLER

The Eleventh Summer

HAMISH HAMILTON

LONDON

11362.

First published in Great Britain 1985
by Hamish Hamilton Ltd
Garden House 57–59 Long Acre London WC2E 9JZ

Copyright © 1985 by Carlo Gébler

British Library Cataloguing in Publication Data
Gébler, Carlo
  The eleventh summer.
  I. Title
  823'.914[F]   PR6057.E/
  ISBN 0-241-11436-5

Typeset by Computape (Pickering) Ltd
Printed in Great Britain by
St Edmundsbury Press, Bury St Edmunds, Suffolk

To my mother

Prologue

He woke up but kept his eyes closed. What had he been dreaming? It would be auspicious to remember. Outside in the garden he could hear sprinklers turning, sous, sous, sous . . . casting water on the parched earth.

He had been back in Ireland in the gardens of a country house. It had been a wet Sunday afternoon. Everywhere there had been rhododendrons dripping from the rain and the paths of red earth had been strewn with huge puddles reflecting the clouds in the sky. He had been waiting for his mother. She had not arrived. He had gone and asked someone when she would come and had been told it would be hours, perhaps days. . . .

The alarm clock began to ring and the rest of the dream, whatever it was, vanished like a minnow darting away underwater. He rolled over and squinted at the clock sitting on his desk, out of reach. It was eight a.m. He felt disinclined to get up. He wanted to ponder the dripping rhododendrons and he entertained the vague hope that perhaps, if he concentrated hard enough, the dream would return. Then he reminded himself there was still packing to do. He threw back the sheets and rose to his feet. As he turned off the alarm he noticed it was faintly chilly.

After he had washed and dressed, he lifted his suitcase onto the end of his bed and began to pile in the remaining items. He had often meant to return but had been putting it off for years. He had always known that his father would have disapproved of him if he had and he had not felt like incurring his wrath over that issue when there were other, more important issues to fight for. Then his father had died and two months later a long weekend's holiday had come up at work. There was nothing to stop him. He had bought the ticket one lunchtime on his way back from the pub. He clicked the suitcase shut and checked the label. Paul Weismann, he read, and the details of his flight to Shannon.

It was time to leave. He carried his suitcase into the common hallway, closed his front door and double-locked it. As he dropped the keys into his pocket he suddenly wondered if he had not perhaps forgotten something. Did he have his ticket? He put his hand to his

1

inside pocket. Yes, it was there. And his wallet? He took it out and flicked it open. Everything was there. Behind the perspex port-hole was a picture of his mother, a young girl in a check shirt, combing her hair and laughing. What about maps? He thought he had put them in but could he be one hundred percent certain? He knelt down and laid the suitcase flat on the ground. It was ridiculous but anxiety was anxiety. If he did not do it straight away he would only end up doing it down in the street, as he knew from past experience. He undid the catches. The maps were in the corner bound with a rubber band. He quickly rummaged through the other contents, assured himself that everything was there and shut the case again.

Walking towards his car he noticed a young girl of about ten standing nearby. Across her shoulders stretched a broom-stick like a yoke and her arms were hanging over it. He remembered he had once seen a cowboy film in which the hero had carried his Winchester rifle in this way.

He dropped his suitcase onto the pavement. From being cold in the early morning the day had gone to being overcast and humid. He opened the boot and stowed his suitcase. As he slammed the lid he noticed the little girl was staring at him. He wiped away the sweat above his mouth.

'Hello,' he said, in his friendliest tone of voice.

'There's a cat under your car mister, I was waiting here to warn you.'

He knelt down on the grimy pavement. Underneath the rear axle a black cat lay on its side.

'Hey!' he called.

The cat lifted his head and regarded him with green eyes.

'Shoo! Go on!' he continued loudly and thumped the side of the door.

The cat stretched back on the tarmac. He climbed into the car and turned on the engine. A couple of revs, he thought, and that should scare it away.

As he climbed out again he noticed the girl had a rabbit embroidered on her dress chewing a carrot between prominent front teeth. He knelt down again. The cat was sitting on its haunches.

'Shoo!' he called. 'Shoo!' But the animal would not move.

He dusted off his knees and pressed the accelerator three more times. The engine roared and a cloud of black smoke drifted from the exhaust pipe.

As he went to bend down again the little girl spoke.

2

'That little black kitten, he run off mister. He run across the road. He's under that red car there.'

He looked across but there was no sign of the troublesome creature.

'I'm going to keep an eye on him over there now. Is he your cat mister?'

'No, he isn't.'

As she crossed the road the chord around her waist swayed at her side.

'Goodbye and thank you.'

'Byeee,' she shouted back.

He settled into the leather driver's seat. His car was an old Morris Oxford. It went slowly, it was like a tank to drive and it was outrageously heavy on petrol. None the less, when collectors had offered to buy it, as had happened once or twice, ridiculous of him as he knew it was, he had always declined. The truth of the matter was he was more than just 'used to it'; he was sentimentally attached.

He pipped the horn as he pulled out. The young girl waved nonchalantly. He proceeded down the street. Stucco façades and fluted columns glided by. He felt strangely light-headed. A picture of the old gates floated up before him and he heard them clanging in their peculiarly mournful way. Not since those first months back in London had he remembered them and now, twenty years afterwards, they came back as clearly as if he had only left a week before. The gates opened and he saw their avenue snaking ahead through a sea of long grass, ragwort and thistles. At the end stood the Red House with the grape-coloured copper beeches shimmering behind. In Black's field to the left there were sheep bleating, their little black feet clipping the sun-baked earth. . . .

Suddenly he noticed he was stopped before a roundabout. It was the last one before the motorway. With his thoughts elsewhere he had been driving automatically. The traffic lights went green. He swung around Cherry Blossom Corner and settled into the slow lane. Direction signs appeared by the roadside. The carriageway rose and narrowed to two lanes. By the old Lucozade clock he saw that he was in good time. The tradenames 'Beecham' and 'Brylcreem' flashed by. The sky overhead was a grey haze. Pictures from that time of his life that had ended when he had come to London began to come one after the other. . . . He saw their front garden and the ornamental stone pineapples on their pedestals; granny straining beetroot over the drain outside the kitchen door, reddish

3

steam rising up, and the dogs Lassie and Rover, aroused by the smell of the vegetable, whining nearby; the light dusting of flour on the kitchen floor after the afternoon's baking; grandfather snoring in the breakfast room, sunlight slanting on his face and all the pages of the *Irish Independent* scattered on the floor around him like fallen leaves; and finally himself, standing in short trousers with water running down his neck, dragging a comb through his unruly hair. . . .

Sunlight fell on the suburbs and the factories stretching on either side of him. He looked into the distance where the road curved towards the sky and imagined himself stepping into the picture and standing beside his eleven-year-old self. A whole morning and afternoon of travelling stretched ahead of him and he could think of nothing better than to pass the time with reveries of the sort which had, quite unexpectedly, offered themselves to him. It was simply a matter of settling back and waiting to see what happened.

Chapter One

He stood in the Blue Room combing his hair. He had just wet it under the cold tap in the bathroom; the hot water tap was not working as usual. As he pulled the comb through the tangles in an attempt to make it lie down, little droplets spotted his lapels.

Reflected in the mirror he could see all of the room behind; blue walls the colour of the summer's sky on granny's cornflower packets; a wallpaper border of red roses running underneath the ceiling; and two big Vono bedsteads standing in each corner. Granny slept in one and he slept in the other. Under granny's bed there was a green plastic bucket that always smelt salty. That was where they peed at night rather than using the water closet next door to grandfather's bedroom. He was such a light sleeper any movement nearby was in danger of waking him.

Between the beds stood a huge wardrobe with a creaking door and a freckled mirror. This was the home of all the clothes granny had brought back from New York in her fashionable days during the twenties. Her hats lived on top. One of these was a Robin Hood hat and had a long brown feather which could be pulled out of its holder. When he was alone in the house he used to take it out of the box, lie on the bed and stroke himself with it, whilst thinking of cousin Philomena. Earlier that summer he had inveigled her to remove her clothes and had discovered that she was curiously different, with strange folds of pink flesh and the mysterious crease between. This had roused an urgency in him which he did not understand.

'Paul, it'll soon be time to go.' It was granny calling from downstairs.

He looked in the mirror one last time. His jacket was grey and cut like a blazer with matching short trousers. Father had bought the suit for him and he had worn it at mother's funeral. The silvery buttons were gleaming, granny having shone them the night before. He put down the comb, strands of hair trapped in its teeth, and ran out.

When he got down to the kitchen he found granny standing by the kitchen window.

'Oh don't you look nice,' she said. 'Let's see you from the back.'

Turning full circle he smelt cabbage boiling on the Aga and the distinctive smell of the anthracite they burnt. It was an interesting smell but it made him itch behind the eyes.

'Will you do old granny a favour and thread the needle for her?'

'Third time lucky,' he said when he finally got the blunted yarn through the eye.

He clambered onto the wooden chair and lifted his arm. She dropped the wallet into his pocket and began to sew it along one side with wide, big stitches.

'Do you promise you'll be careful?'

'Yes.'

'And not give your money away?'

'No.'

'And if you take your money out, you'll let no one see.'

'Yes . . . I mean . . . no!'

'Your wallet is sewn in so you won't lose your money.'

She cut the thread and tied the loose ends into a cluster of knots.

'Promise to be a good boy?'

'Yes.'

She held him by the shoulders and stared into his eyes.

'Look after grandfather? We don't want him getting ill again?'

'Yes.'

'Promise?'

He nodded emphatically.

'Good boy.'

He jumped down and ran to the Fyson's Salts tin on the window ledge. Inside, in addition to the orange ten-shilling note which he owned, he found a florin which had not been there before.

'How did the two shillings get there?' he asked.

'That's for you lovey, so you don't have to break into your ten shillings.'

She was always springing little surprises on him like that. He twisted round and put the note in the compartment marked 'Bank Notes' and the coin in the side purse which shut with a popper.

There was a knock at the kitchen window. He looked up. It was grandfather in his best dark suit.

'Bring up my field glasses,' he shouted through the glass. 'I'll be waiting in the yard.'

Paul lifted the binoculars down from the dresser. The case left a shape in the dust like a stretched kidney.

Granny kissed him goodbye. 'You will look after grandfather? We don't want anything happening to him!'

'Don't worry,' he called blithely and disappeared through the kitchen door.

He ran across the concrete flag to the back gate, passed the fieldglasses through the bottom rung and laid them in the long grass. The gate was rusty though it had been pale green once. Climbing over he caught a glimpse of granny waving from the kitchen window. She mouthed something which he could not hear.

The path to the yard stretched ahead of him, covered with black cinders. On the right was the chopping block, the ground around it strewn with wooden chips like the feathers left after a fox has eaten a chicken. Further on sprawled the rotting oak, felled by lightning years before. Paul picked up the red leather case and started to run.

Grandfather was waiting in the yard with Joseph, the farm-hand. Joseph was a thick man who smelt sourly of his sweat and had a shiny complexion that reminded Paul of an uncooked sausage. Because of his short-sightedness Joseph wore gold-rimmed spectacles which misted up when he got hot. He was said to be retarded. Paul's grandfather paid him £5.0s.0d a week. The men were not talking but staring at the ground and tracing nervous circles with their feet on the hard, dry earth.

'I fetched your fieldglasses.'

His grandfather took the glasses and hung them round his scrawny neck.

'The right word is brought.'

A car horn honked and their three heads swivelled. Through the gate from the back avenue nosed Mr McKenna's Austin Cambridge, a green horse-box hitched behind it. It had not rained for a fortnight and so the yard was ribbed with ruts. As Mr McKenna bumped slowly across, car and horse-box rose and fell like a boat at sea.

'You'd think he'd a load of eggs the speed he's going,' muttered grandfather.

Mr McKenna got out of his car and closed the door after himself.

'Ten to one he locks it,' said grandfather.

'Good afternoon Mr O'Berne,' called Mr McKenna.

'Hello there.'

Mr McKenna picked his way towards them in newly polished shoes.

'Nice day for a spin,' he said. Under his heavy jacket Mr McKenna wore a woollen waistcoat with wooden buttons. The sun

7

was hot but not Mr McKenna. At all times he seemed unaffected by the temperature around him. 'Will it be a winner?' he continued shyly.

'Are you thinking of having a bet?' retorted grandfather.

'Well, not exactly.'

'You're not going to bet on my magnificent horse?'

'I wouldn't say . . . that. . . at this stage.'

Mr McKenna moved a stone with his foot.

'Well I shan't be having a bet,' said grandfather. 'It's more in the nature of a test run today. We're just letting her stretch her legs. But don't come whining to me when she romps home at a hundred-to-eight and say that I didn't tell you to put any money on her.'

Mr McKenna, still staring at the ground, went bright red and looked as though he heartily wished he had not started the conversation.

Grandfather took his fob-watch out of his waistcoat pocket. It was an American watch; with the Statue of Liberty engraved on the back and a swarm of swallows on the front clustered round a glass port-hole. This watch, Paul knew, was called a half-hunter, because a man on horseback could tell the time without opening it by merely looking through the port-hole.

'We'd better be moving.'

Joseph lifted the halter from the grass and went into the derelict building that ran along one side of the yard. The four crumbling walls and a doorway with a cracked lintel over the top which was inscribed AD 1649 were all that remained of the large house that had once stood there. Grandfather had lived in it before he had been married, until it burnt down one winter's night. It was rumoured that he had set fire to it in a fit of drunken rage although he insisted it had been an accident. Before grandfather's time landed gentry had lived in this house. It had had a ballroom and everyone important in the district had gone there for the dances. Sometimes, on still summer nights, Paul was certain he could hear ghostly music drifting down from the ruin.

Joseph emerged with a huge four-year-old chestnut. She had white socks and a dark mane.

'Good looking animal, wouldn't you say?'

'She is,' concurred Mr McKenna.

Whilst Joseph held the halter, grandfather rubbed his cheek against her dark, warm coat and murmured endearments. He had a way with horses, especially the big ones that raced.

'Come here and say "hello".'

8

Grandfather waved Paul forward with his scrawny hand. Paul noticed his skin was blueish in the sunlight and he could half-make out the dark outlines of his bones underneath. These were surprisingly frail and almost bird-like.

'She won't bite. Go on! Stroke her!'

As he touched Red River Rose, a fly landed on her flank and her whole body shivered. It was like receiving a small electric shock. He jumped back and fell over a rut the size of a boot-scraper.

'Get up,' grandfather shouted. 'Don't make such a fool of yourself.'

He stood up and dusted off the earth from his haunches.

'Don't mind the earth, you ass, come here.'

The bottom of his back was hurting and his face was glowing with shame and fear.

'She won't harm you,' said grandfather. 'Whenever you have a tumble,' he continued, 'you should get straight back on the horse. The same thing applies here.'

With beating heart, he reached out and touched her on the neck. 'Good horsie. Good Red River Rose,' he murmured.

'You see, there was no need to make all that fuss,' said grandfather.

Her nostrils, Paul noticed, were the colour of mushroom soup and filled with tiny hairs which had beads of moisture on their ends. They trembled with her breath like sea anemones swaying under water.

'Now make yourself scarce,' ordered grandfather. Paul backed away.

When he climbed into the car he found it was baking hot, and he sat suspended on his knuckles above the back seat. He waited until his arms got tired, then lowered himself down. Although the seat was still hot, he knew it would become bearable. Then he wound down the back windows with handles that were like hot spoons.

A susurrus of voice and hoof drifted in as the men corraled Red River Rose into her box. He dug his hands into the crack at the back of the seat and felt around for the change which he knew sometimes fell down there. This time his luck was out.

The ramp closed with a muffled thump and the retaining bolts dropped into place. In the box, Red River rose trod warily on her boards.

'"Okey-dokey," as the Yank said – let's go.' Grandfather was in high spirits as he settled into the front seat.

Mr McKenna checked that his door was shut, made a slight adjustment to his hat and turned the key in the ignition.

9

'Goodbye,' called Joseph humbly.

As Mr McKenna did a wide, bumping sweep of the yard, Paul twisted round in his seat to wave back. Through the back window he saw Joseph standing in front of the derelict mansion, a sad expression on his face. In the past Joseph had always gone along to the races with grandfather, assisted with the grooming and helped parade the horses around the paddock. However, on the previous occasion he had brought disgrace on himself. By keeping his ears open and pretending to be stupid, Paul had been able to piece the whole story together. On that particular day, grandfather had gone to race a filly called Green Fields in whom he had high hopes. Large sums had been placed at the bookie's. Unhappily, Green Fields had refused to move and when the race finished she was still at the starting post. With this humiliation for an excuse, grandfather had run to the refreshment tent and drunk a bottle of brandy. It had been his first drink for four years and Joseph had been unable to stop him even though he had known it was expected of him. Come evening, crying and repentant, Joseph had returned home with Green Fields. Grandfather had not been with him; he had gone off with two farmers. A week later word came that he was lodging in a hotel in Athlone. Granny had gone with Uncle James to collect him. When they arrived they found him lying naked under the bedcovers shaking with delirium tremens, empty brandy bottles rattling around in the bed with him. He had destroyed the linoleum floor by stubbing his cigarettes out on it and mired the sink and the headboard of the bed with excrement and phlegm. The hotel management were outraged and had insisted that none of the staff could clean the room. Granny had had to pay them two pounds so that a man could be specially brought in to do the job. Filled with shame they had brought him back by taxi and put him to bed. After that granny had kept him home for several months and now he was being allowed out again, only this time, as Paul realised, it was he who was going along as chaperone, Joseph being regarded as unreliable. Granny herself would not go and never had because, as she had explained to him, she was allergic to race horses. They made her sick and brought her out in a rash.

Mr McKenna edged up to the gates leading to the back avenue or the Bog Road as it was called.

'Buckets of room,' called grandfather though he was not looking out of the window.

Mr McKenna swallowed hard and gripped the wheel tighter.

As the car drove away, Paul continued to wave back, moved by the guilty wish to make up to Joseph because he was going in his place. Then the car rounded a bend and Joseph and the yard disappeared from sight behind a leafy screen of trees.

Outside the gateway to the race-track sat a tinker woman with thick, rubbery skin and hooded eyes, a dirty child asleep on her breast with thumb in mouth. In the shoe-box in front of her lay a few dull coppers.

'Look at that! Looking for something for nothing!' said grandfather.

Clack, clack, clack – the car went across the cattle-grid and through the gates, the hinges of which were rusty with dark brown stains on the piers.

'Yes, the country's going to the dogs,' Mr McKenna retorted.

Inside the gate, a woman in a headscarf was tacking a red oil-cloth to a trestle table. Beside her, a young boy unloaded crates of lemonade and cherryade from a van. A row of tick-tack men were setting up their blackboards on stilts. Two workmen slowly pushed a trolley loaded with chairs. A vendor unwrapped oranges from tissue paper and laid them in immaculate rows.

'Oranges, best oranges. . . .'

In the car park near the Course Offices they found Mickey waiting. He was sitting on a rusty drum chewing a piece of grass. Mickey was fat and his bottom seemed to spill over the top of his trousers. Under his arms he was wet. Mickey was a cousin of the jockey, Liam. It was his job to groom the horse, saddle her and lead her round the paddock.

'Mickey?' called grandfather.

'Yes, Mr O'Berne.'

'Where's Liam?'

'He's in the weighing room,' said Mickey, squinting and leaning with his big hands on the side of the car. 'Doesn't like the sun. His skin's too soft. Too white,' Mickey chuckled.

Grandfather opened the door. 'Don't stray!' he called to his grandson in the back.

Paul sat in the car, heard the ramp dropping gently and Red River Rose being backed down.

'Come on my beauty. You've arrived . . . ' coaxed Mickey.

Mr McKenna opened his book and started to read. It was a detective novel with a girl and a gun and a man on its garish cover. A book-marker from one of the Missionary Societies peeped out from its middle. Mr McKenna would spend the afternoon engrossed in the book. Paul knew this from the times Mr McKenna

11

had driven him and granny to the seaside. Once he arrived, Mr McKenna never moved from his car or strayed from his book.

'You run well today. You be a good horse. . . .'

Grandfather stood close to Red River Rose and held his open hand under her moving lips.

'Treat her with kid gloves, Mickey!'

'Don't worry Mr O'Berne.'

Grandfather returned to the car.

'Adios, Mr McKenna.'

Mr McKenna looked up from his book.

'Good luck,' he said.

'Come on, Paul,' called grandfather.

Paul opened the door and jumped from the shaded car into the sun.

Grandfather set off across the car park at a brisk pace. He had been a champion walker in his youth and still had a habit of hurrying everywhere. Paul followed breathlessly, picking his way around the numerous pot-holes. The rain water which usually filled these had evaporated in the heat, leaving only wet, warm mud in the holes. On the steps on the far side of the car park lay an empty brown beer bottle.

The sign on the door said 'Weighing and Changing Room'. The words made Paul immediately anxious. What if there were a naked man inside? Where should he look?

'Shall I wait here, grandfather?'

'You will not. You'll be polite and come in and say hullo.'

Standing in the entrance were large weighing scales, all gleaming white enamel except for the dull aluminium footplate. The room behind was long and dark with benches on either side. There were curling double hooks sticking out from the walls and at the end there was a shower. Paul strained to hear the sound of running water and was grateful there was none to be heard.

Liam the jockey was sitting in the corner.

'Ah, Liam! Hiding from us are you?'

'Mr O'Berne, I didn't hear you come in.' He cupped the cigarette and stood up immediately.

Liam was immaculate in a blue suit, red tie and gold tie-pin with a green stone set in the middle. He smelt of soap.

'Say hullo, Paul,' said grandfather, propelling the boy forward.

Shyly Paul grasped Liam's hand and looked up. He saw that everything about Liam was broad at the top and tapered down-wards: broad forehead, a small mouth and pointed chin; wide shoulders and a slim waist; spindly legs and tiny feet. Liam's grip, Paul noticed, was surprisingly weak.

'She's a strong horse,' said grandfather urgently, 'but she doesn't know how to pace herself.'

Paul let go of Liam's hand and retreated a step.

'All dash and no follow through,' grandfather continued.

Liam nodded.

'Hold her back at the start. Let her get the feel of the turf. Let her get used to the crowds; then let her go!'

'We'll have a bullseye today. Don't you worry . . .' boasted Liam.

Paul wandered back to the entrance and gingerly stepped on the weighing scales. The footplate shifted below him like thin ice and the needle swept upwards.

'Hey, that's for jockeys not for pipsqueaks!' grandfather called.

'Don't mind that,' interceded Liam. 'How much do you weigh lad?'

Liam took a final puff of his cigarette and then killed it with his thumb-nail. The butt went back into the packet.

'I weigh four stone, twelve pounds and three and a quarter ounces.'

'Well, Liam,' asked grandfather, 'will he make a jockey, do you think?'

'Does he like his grub?'

'Will he make a jockey as good as you?'

'Who can tell? Only God in Heaven.'

Paul followed his grandfather into a toilet. It had a red tiled floor and smelt of antiseptic. There was a tinker boy bending over one of the deep white sinks. He was scooping water and gulping it down. Beside him stood another young tinker, gazing at himself in the mirror, and as grandfather and grandson passed by, the tinkers stared after them. Paul felt embarrassed to be wearing what was obviously a new suit. He put his hand into his side pocket and curled his fingers around his wallet for safe keeping.

When he came to pee, Paul found he could not. He wanted to go into a closet but that would have shown the tinker boys that he was nervous. He buttoned up his trousers and went back to the basins, selecting the one that was furthest from where they were lurking. Greyish soap trickled from the dispenser into his hand. It felt gritty. Out of the corner of his eye he saw he was being watched. Grandfather appeared beside him then. He heard footfalls behind. Looking in the mirror he saw the tinker boys approaching. His heart began to beat.

'Excuse me mister, could you lend us some money? It'll bring you good fortune.'

It was the thirsty one speaking. He had black, curly hair with bits of straw in it.

'Leave us in peace, damn you,' cursed grandfather.

'Just a shilling for a cup of tea. We've been on the road all night. It'll bring you luck, mister,' the tinker repeated.

'You people have plenty of money, so don't come begging to me.'

'We have not, sir, and we're thirsty.'

He held out his grubby hand.

'It'll bring you luck.'

'Out of my way,' urged grandfather.

With his dripping hands he pushed the curly haired tinker aside and went over to the towel dispenser. 'You'll get nothing from me!' he said with a scowl.

The tinker spat on the floor. 'May you have bad luck then,' he said, and turned towards the door, followed by his comrade.

The room echoed as grandfather pulled down a length of clean towel.

'Yes, bad luck to you,' shouted the other who had so far been silent.

As they left, the tinker boys slammed the outside door with all their might which made the mirrors on the walls shake.

Paul was left with an unpleasant feeling in his stomach, like he would get at school when a fight was brewing.

Mickey and Red River Rose were third into the paddock. Leaning on his elbows, Paul squinted past grandfather along the rails. They were lined with spectators, many of whom were holding their race-cards over their eyes to shield them from the sun. In the midst of the noisy race course, the paddock was a calm, quiet place. Comments, when they were made, were quietly spoken and followed by long lapses of silence. The spectators were locked into their private worlds of evaluation, prediction and intuition.

As Mickey approached, Paul tried to catch his eye but was studiously ignored. Mickey's face was broad like Liam's, tapering to a point and covered with freckles, big irregular ones; he even had freckles on his eyelids. From the groom Paul glanced up at Liam astride the big chestnut mare. His legs were hitched up and he looked as though he were squatting on her back. Liam wore his black hat pushed back from his wide, white forehead at a slightly jaunty angle, and his silk shirt fluttered in the breeze like a flag.

Red River Rose passed by in slow motion, her feet sending up little flurries of dust from the ground. Other horses followed and the paddock soon filled up. It was the major race of the afternoon, and there were twenty runners. As he watched, Paul began to feel tremendously excited. His own grandfather's horse was about to race before the crowds. It then occurred to him that he might place a bet. He turned around and looked across the milling crowds to where a row of bookmakers was standing on little boxes with their faded and worn blackboards beside them upon which they chalked up the odds. Even though the sun was beating down, many were wearing black overcoats and some were even wearing bowler hats. Paul wondered if this had anything to do with their reputation of making 'hasty exits'. In the end, because of this, he decided against laying a bet. He felt with his moist fingers the ten-shilling note safe in his wallet and was pleased.

'Wait here and don't move,' said grandfather, surprising him.

Paul watched as his grandfather pushed his way through the crowds to a red-faced man in the middle of the row. After a moment's conversation, he seemed to hand over money and in return received something which he then placed behind his fob-watch. From where he stood, Paul could not make out what it was. As grandfather made his way back to the paddock, the tick-tack man rubbed his blackboard clean and chalked up something new. A flurry of arm-waving followed.

'A man's business is a man's business,' said grandfather leaning back on the rails.

Paul nodded.

'Now I don't want you carrying tales to your grandmother. Do you understand?'

'Yes,' agreed Paul.

'If she wins, I'll splash out on you.'

He nodded again.

There was an announcement over the tannoy about the race starting in fifteen minutes' time.

Holding him by the arm, grandfather careered down the steps of the stand.

'Excuse me! Do you mind!' shouted a big woman whose hat had been knocked askew.

'I'm sorry,' said Paul as they flew by. Should he have explained that they had a horse running in the next race? he thought, but by then it was too late.

At the bottom they squeezed through the crowd and found a

place at the rails. It was close to the white pole with a circle on top which marked the finish. Behind the winning post, the judge sat in a box drinking tea from a thermos flask. Down the other end of the track, a huddle of horses were being cajoled into their starting positions. At last Paul could rest. He took off his jacket and laid it over the rails. It was very hot. He looked up. The sky was blue, deep blue above him and fading to a lighter blue towards the horizon. As he stared up he imagined it went on forever and he was filled with a sense of promise which he could not put into words. In the distance lay a line of hills. They were dark green on top and lighter green and shades of dun lower down, where they were divided into fields for cultivation. A cloud passed and a huge shadow that looked like a whale moved over them at enormous speed. He remembered being told by his father that in the stratosphere, great winds could roar whilst on earth all would be calm. But when larks hung in the air and sang, were they buffeted? he wondered.

'Paul!' A voice broke his thoughts.

Grandfather tapped him on the shoulder and pointed down the track. At the far end a couple of men in white coats stood beside the horses in their stalls. Suddenly the men moved aside, the horses moved and the crowd began to murmur. The race had started. Paul was completely taken by surprise. He had expected them to start behind a white ribbon and a gun to be fired.

Grandfather raised his fieldglasses to his eyes.

'Come on, my beauty,' he whispered. 'Don't let me down.'

All Paul could see was a huddle of horses, a couple already lagging behind. What was happening? he wondered. Who was winning?

'Careful, Liam. Careful. Hold her. Don't let her go,' said grandfather anxiously.

'Come on Black Boy,' someone screeched. It was a man in a double-breasted suit. Paul turned, and saw that the sinews of the man's neck were standing up under his skin like wires.

'Come on, Mink Coat. Come on you lovely thing,' a third voice bellowed.

Everyone on the stand was calling and bawling, urging and promising the earth in return for victory.

The horses drew closer and the sound of their hooves grew louder.

'That's it, Liam. Now's your moment. Don't be shy. . . . Let her go you imbecile. . . .' The pitch of grandfather's voice rose as he yelled against the crowd.

From the incoherent huddle racing towards them, one horse separated itself and started to surge forward. It was Paul's impres-

16

sion that this horse had sprouted wings and was flying along. As the horse drew closer his heart soared; it was Red River Rose.

'Red River Rose. Red River Rose.' There were others calling her name too.

'Red River Rose, come on,' he piped himself, his voice reedy amidst the roar of the horse-throated crowd.

'Yes, Liam,' grandfather shouted, 'by Jesus you'll be a rich man.'

The horses were quite close now. Their hooves were battering the turf, making a tremendous noise, and Paul could feel vibrations from the earth shivering up his legs.

'Come on,' Paul called again.

She was far ahead of the rest of the pack and increasing the distance with every stride. The winning post was not far away and victory seemed hers, even if she slowed to a canter or a trot, Paul thought. The inevitability of triumph with still some distance to run was the most wonderful sensation.

Then it happened: Red River Rose jolted and seemed to stand still in the air as if she had collided with an invisible stone wall. Her legs buckled beneath her and her head twisted upwards and sideways. A moment later she crumpled to the ground throwing Liam towards the distant rails. There was a murmur of dismay from the crowd.

'Blasted hell!' shouted grandfather.

The pack surged past and through the blur Paul saw their jockey scrambling to safety. Grandfather ducked under the rails and started to run across the turf. Paul scuttled after. Grandfather ran stiffly, waving his arms about uselessly, his fieldglasses bumping against his side and his hat falling to the ground. Paul passed the hat lying neatly crown upwards and ran on to where Red River Rose lay whimpering on the turf. Her neck was twisted at an odd angle to the rest of her body and her head rested on the earth like an immoveable dead weight. Liam knelt beside the horse, touching her neck. He had lost his hat but retained his whip which hung useless by a strap from his wrist. His silk shirt was torn at the button-holes and stained green by the grass at the shoulders. His eyes were bloodshot and his cheeks were streaked with tears.

'I'm sorry Mr O'Berne,' Liam stammered, straightening up. 'I think her neck's broken.'

Grandfather shouted something indecipherable, his eyes bulging from their sockets. He took off his fieldglasses and hurled them onto the turf. Paul remembered there were spectators watching and felt uncomfortable.

17

A man came running up carrying a small black bag. It was the course vet. He nodded towards grandfather and knelt down by Red River Rose.

'Is there any hope?' pleaded grandfather.

The vet ran his hands over the mare's neck and stood up. He did not even open his bag.

'I'm sorry,' said the vet, 'her neck's broken. She'll have to be put down.'

'But you haven't examined her properly,' said grandfather. 'What about X-rays?'

'I'm sorry. Her neck is broken. We can't leave her in this sort of agony for a second longer.'

The vet opened his bag and took out a revolver which he put in his pocket. Then he returned to the bag and started rummaging around inside.

'Damnation,' he muttered finally to himself and clicked the bag shut.

He beckoned a steward with a wave of his hand. 'Come here,' he called.

The steward ran over and the vet whispered something in his ear.

'Yes, sir,' replied the steward confidentially.

The steward turned round and started to run up the track and the vet sidled up to grandfather with an obsequious expression on his face.

'There's going to be a slight delay,' he apologised. 'Whoever packed my bag forgot to include the ammunition. The steward's gone for it. I'm very sorry.'

Weeping and blowing his nose, grandfather nodded. 'Are you certain that there's nothing can be done?'

'I'm absolutely certain, sir.'

For want of something to do, Paul wandered back to where grandfather's hat lay on the grass. At the rails close by, a crowd of onlookers had gathered. Their expressions were a strange mixture of sympathy and disgust. They blame grandfather for what happened, he thought as he bent down to pick up the hat. The idea made him anxious and, as he retraced his steps, he was certain he could feel their eyes drilling into his back. At the end, he could not stop himself breaking into a nervous run.

A tractor drove up with two men on it. They jumped down and started to unravel some sort of tackle from the back. The metal chains made a dull thump as they fell on the earth. Red River Rose

18

jerked with fright and rolled her eyes. Liam knelt down and stroked her side.

'There, there,' he said soothingly. 'You'll be all right in a minute.'

Red River Rose shrieked again and struggled to get to her feet. It was as if she knew what fate awaited her. Grandfather sobbed quietly. The vet lit a cigarette. He was a youngish man, informally dressed. His jacket did not match his trousers and his hair was longer than orthodox and curled over his collar. He had a slight pot belly. At last the steward arrived, carrying a small cardboard box which rattled as he ran.

'Thank God,' exclaimed the vet.

He opened the box and counted out two bullets. The tips of the bullets were dark silver and their cases brassy yellow. He took the pistol out of his pocket and opened the chamber.

'What about him? Shouldn't someone take him away?' asked the vet, pointing at Paul.

'Come on,' said Liam, putting his arm over his shoulder. 'You shouldn't see this.'

After taking about a dozen paces, Paul shrugged his shoulders and slipped from Liam's grasp. As he turned around he saw the vet was pointing his gun at the horse's forehead.

'Don't look,' whispered Liam, reaching over to cover Paul's eyes with his hand. But before Liam could reach him, the vet pulled the trigger. The gunshot was unexpectedly dull in the open country. Red River Rose twitched as though she had received an electric shock, and a small flurry of blood leapt from her forehead into the air.

'You shouldn't have watched,' said Liam. 'But there's no harm I suppose. You're grown up enough, aren't you?'

The vet bent down by Red River Rose and felt with his fingers at the bottom of her neck. A moment later he stood up, opened the chamber of the gun and took out the second bullet. Red River Rose was dead. The vet nodded at the tractor-men waiting nearby.

They drove up at quite a speed, the tackle dragging behind. It made a strange jingling sound as it bounced across the turf. When they reached the carcass, they braked hard and jumped down. At the ends of the tackle there were hessian-coloured pads, and the men started to attach these under and around the horse. Grandfather kept getting in their way so the vet took him aside and led him over to Paul and Liam. Across the turf, Paul could hear the men's muttered exhortations:

'That's it. Lift her there. I'll take the weight. . . .'

19

'Did you ever come across such a heavy horse?'

When they finished, the driver asked the vet what time it was.

'Four o'clock,' the vet replied.

'Jesus! We'd better get a move on,' said the driver.

They all jumped onto the tractor and the driver started it up. As the vehicle crept forward the slack chains of the tackle sprung into the air and went rigid with a clack and the large black tyres skidded on the grass. For a moment, it looked as though Red River Rose might be too heavy. Then the driver accelerated and slowly the carcass started to move.

'Thank you lads,' the vet called.

The men on the tractor waved back.

'Goodbye,' said the vet to grandfather and Liam.

'Goodbye,' replied Liam.

Grandfather said something but it was inaudible.

As the vet turned and walked away, the tractor did a wide circle across the track in front of them. For a moment Red River Rose was quite close and Paul saw her tongue was hanging out. It was big and red and left a trail of saliva on the grass.

'The best horse I ever had,' moaned grandfather.

The tractor sped away from them, passing the winning post and continued up the track. Red River Rose bounced behind, the chains of the tackle sending up lumps of earth and grass. At the top, where the track curled to the left, there was a gap in the rails on the right. The tractor swept through and disappeared out of sight behind a cluster of official buildings. For some time afterwards the three of them stood rooted to the spot, staring at the gap in the rails. Paul knew it was a moment he would never forget. Over the tannoy, a voice announced the next race. It was time to go. Grandfather blew his nose and wiped his eyes.

'The fieldglasses,' said Paul, pointing to where they lay. 'I'll fetch them.'

'No, no. I will,' interrupted Liam.

On his spindly legs Liam ran over to the middle of the track and picked them up. As he hurried back, he wiped away the earth and grass stuck to the lens. When they were clean he put the glasses back in their case.

'Mr O'Berne, your fieldglasses,' he said.

Grandfather said nothing but dropped his head forward. Liam hung them around his neck.

'I'm sorry,' said Liam. It made Paul uncomfortable to see an adult trying to wheedle forgiveness like a child.

20

'It's a bitter blow; to lose her in her prime....' But before he had finished his sentence, grandfather turned and walked away with slow, shuffling steps like an old man.

Paul collected his coat from the railing and followed Liam and grandfather up the stairs towards the exit. The stand was beginning to fill up in anticipation of the next race. On either side, people stared at them and murmured. They were a strange sight; a jockey in a torn shirt; an old man sniffling into his handkerchief; and a young boy in a suit, carrying a grown man's hat.

From the stand they went to the Track offices. There were formalities to be dealt with and the disposal of the remains to be arranged. Grandfather and Liam went in, leaving Paul outside. He sat down on the steps to wait. After a few moments Mickey appeared. He sidled up as if he were frightened.

'Is the boss taking it to heart?' he asked apprehensively.

Paul said that he was.

Mickey sighed heavily and sat down on the step beside him.

'It was a terrible thing to happen. A cruel twist of fate ... ' he continued.

Paul recognised that he was being sympathetic but everything about Mickey irritated him; his plumpness; the smell of his sweat; his incessant tongue; and most of all the way Mickey's shoulders touched his own. He shifted along the wood. There was a silence. Mickey sighed loudly, dug his hand into his pocket and brought out a packet of Woodbines.

'Smoke?'

Paul shook his head.

'I find cigarettes are great to calm the nerves. Have one! Go on! You look like you need one.'

Paul shook his head again and moved still further away.

'If you change your mind, tell me.'

Mickey lit a cigarette and flicked the match away with a flourish.

'It could have been worse,' he continued sagely. 'I suppose that's one way of looking at it. There could have been a nasty pile-up. It could have been several horses then and jockeys too. All in all we got off lightly really.'

Mickey drew deeply on his cigarette and started to blow smoke rings. The blue smoke circles rose upwards, one after the other, to about the level of the guttering, then shuddered and dissolved. Paul was grateful for the silence and as he watched he remembered he had once been taken to a balloonists' rally by his father.

21

A door scraped open and Mickey and Paul jumped up. It was grandfather, with Liam creeping behind.

'Come on,' called grandfather to Paul as he headed towards the steps.

'Goodbye, Liam. Goodbye, Mickey,' cried Paul. He jumped down the four steps and ran after grandfather towards the safety of Mr McKenna and the car.

Paul sat in the boiling back. Grandfather sat in the front passenger seat, crying quietly. Mr McKenna squeezed the wheel, driving with extra care. Mickey had had the good sense to tell him what had happened and Mr McKenna had expressed his condolences at the start of the journey. 'I was sorry to hear your bad news,' he had said. Behind the car the empty horse-box rattled and squeaked and beyond the windows, fields and hedgerows floated by, lit by the sun. It was a still summer's afternoon. Paul looked in the rear-view mirror. As far as he could see, Mr McKenna was staring ahead without blinking, his expression somehow like that of a dog. Grandfather had his hands over his eyes and could not be seen.

After driving for what he judged to be quite a while he heard his grandfather saying, 'Stop!'

'What?' asked Mr McKenna.

Grandfather slapped the cushioned top of the dashboard.

'Stop! Do you hear? Stop over there. You're not deaf, are you?'

Grandfather indicated a gaunt, grey, slate-roofed building standing at a crossroads with a single petrol pump in front of it. Paul realised instantly what sort of a place it was.

'I don't want any lemonade,' he stammered. The words came out without his having to think about them.

'Shut up you little squirt.'

Paul knew Mr McKenna would do nothing to avert the coming disaster, so he turned to God. Dear God, he prayed, let this just be a simple call for nature. But even as he pronounced the words he knew it was useless. Grandfather was going back on the batter and there was nothing he could do to stop him. Ten grown men could not have prevented him so what could he a mere boy do? As the car crept towards the public house, Paul recalled the hotel sink and bed mired with green phlegm and excrement. Would this horror be repeated? He retched and covered his mouth with his hand.

'Park over there!' grandfather ordered, pointing to the spot. Mr McKenna drew up slowly and grandfather jumped out.

'Come on,' he said, rapping on Paul's door. 'You'll have a lemonade.'

Paul crept out and followed him over to the front door.

'Any chance of a man having a drink?' grandfather angrily called and banged with his fist on the wood.

After a considerable pause a man replied from within. 'Hang on,' he shouted.

The muffled sound of bolts being drawn and keys being turned drifted out, and then the door was scraped open by a small balding publican. His black hair grew in a ring around the outside of his head and a tea-towel hung over his shoulder.

'Any chance of a drink?' asked grandfather politely. His voice was calm and reasonable. The publican looked him up and down.

'Yes, I think so,' he said.

The publican stepped aside and grandfather darted in. Paul followed. Beyond the door, he found himself in a short passage. On one wall there hung a picture of a greyhound called 'Master McGrath' and on the other there was an engraving of Robert Emmet and the words 'Ireland's Patriot Martyr' written in copper-plate underneath. The double door to the bar was at the end. Grandfather was already perched on a high-stool and the barman was behind the counter, slowly pulling down the tea-towels which covered the bottles on the shelves. There was a sweet-sour smell of old porter.

'Sit there,' grandfather ordered Paul as he walked in. He pointed at the stool next to him. Paul clambered up. The seat was sticky.

'I'll have a double brandy,' grandfather said.

'Now just hang on!' The barman was tetchy.

'I haven't got all day!'

'A double did you say?'

'Yes. I said a double.'

The barman took a brandy glass down and gave it a wipe.

'Don't mind the glass,' urged grandfather. 'Just give me the drink.'

'As you please.'

The barman put the glass down on the counter and poured in the brandy straight from the bottle.

'What are you having?' grandfather growled.

23

'Nothing,' Paul said. 'I don't think I'm well.'

'Don't be so namby-pamby! Lemonade for the young man,' he called.

The barman slid the glass across the counter. Grandfather lifted it up with his two hands and laid it on his thin wiry lip. He folded his head back and the brown liquid ran forward into his mouth, a little trickle escaping at the edge and dribbling onto the lapel of his jacket. As grandfather drained the glass Paul heard the sound of water spattering softly onto linoleum. He looked down and saw a warm, brackish stream trickling along his legs, running over his polished shoes and dripping onto the floor. He blinked, wondered what was happening and then realised he had wet himself.

The barman set his lemonade down in front of him. He wondered if the barman would notice the salty pee-smell that was already drifting upwards. The thought of this humiliation was worse than his discomfort. Between his legs his warm, wet clothes were rapidly turning cold.

'Another brandy, please,' said grandfather, holding his glass out.

The barman filled his glass and he drank it. Then he drank a third and a fourth and a fifth. . . .

'Another!' demanded grandfather. This was to be his sixth.

'Haven't you had enough?' asked the barman.

'By God I haven't. If I had all the brandy in the country I wouldn't have enough. My heart is broken.'

'This'll be your last, mind you,' said the barman as he poured it out.

Grandfather gulped it down and demanded a seventh.

'I think you've had enough,' said the barman. 'Haven't you got a home to go to?'

'I have a home – of course I have a home. Haven't we got a home, Paul? With granny there waiting for us?'

'Yes,' muttered Paul.

'I think the little fellow's tired,' said the barman.

'He's not tired!' roared grandfather. 'You're not tired, Paul, are you?'

Paul said nothing.

'I think you should bring him home.'

'Another drink,' bellowed grandfather.

'You heard what I said. The last was your last.'

'Another fucking drink I tell you.'

'I'm sorry, you'll have to go! This is an orderly house. I don't tolerate language like that.'

'Give us a fucking drink.'

'I think you should be sensible and go quietly.'

Grandfather jumped to his feet, knocking his stool to the floor. 'If you don't give me a drink I'll take it myself,' he shouted and lurched towards the raised flap that gave entrance to the bar. The barman tried to shut the flap but grandfather was too quick. He caught it with his arm and pushed forward.

'You little arsehole,' grandfather shouted. 'I'd eat you for breakfast.'

The barman retreated and caught his legs on the crate Paul's lemonade had come from. As he toppled back he clutched at a towel on which a dozen upturned glasses were drying.

'Jimmie!' the barman shouted and glasses crashed around him.

Grandfather seized the bottle of brandy from the ledge where it stood and staggered out from behind the counter. At the back of the bar a door opened and Jimmie appeared. He was about four-teen and one of his legs was in a caliper.

'Lock the door,' screamed the barman as he scrambed to his feet. 'Telephone the guards!'

As Jimmie locked the scullery door, the barman darted across the room past grandfather and disappeared through the public entrance, slamming it after himself.

'You're not worth a fucking box of matches,' grandfather shouted after him.

A moment later Paul heard a key turning in the lock of the public entrance. He and grandfather were prisoners, he realised.

Grandfather dropped the brandy cork on the floor and raised the bottle to his lips. As he gulped it back, some of the liquor splattered down his neck and onto his collar. The dark stain was like perspir-ation. Paul climbed down from his stool and went to the window, put his hands in his pockets and lifted away his clammy trousers and sodden underpants from his skin. A wonderful sensation of cooling and drying followed and he went into a sort of numb daze. He began to forget where he was and what had happened. Time passed without his being aware of it. Then he saw a big, burly guard bicycling up the road towards the pub, and he was jolted out of his reverie.

Paul took his hands out of his pockets and turned around. Grandfather was nowhere in sight. From behind the bar he heard a flailing sound.

'Help me,' his grandfather called.

He ran behind the counter. His grandfather was lying on the floor in a stupor and could not get back onto his feet. Paul took hold of his grandfather by the arm and tried to help him up.

The door of the public entrance burst open and the guard and the barman came in. Paul stared at them from behind the bar. He felt like a thief caught in the act.

'That your car outside?' asked the guard in a high-pitched voice.

'Yes,' said Paul.

The guard turned to the barman. 'Any damage done?' he asked.

'Not as far as I can see.'

'Right!' said the guard. 'Let's put him in the car. What's your name?'

'Paul.'

'Out of my way, Paul.'

The guard squatted down and gathered up grandfather, lifting him to his feet in one easy movement.

'What about paying?' asked the barman.

'Oh yes.' The guard propped grandfather against the bar and pulled his wallet out of his pocket.

'He had a bottle of brandy,' said the barman. 'That's fourteen bob.'

'You're out of luck I'm afraid.' The guard held open the wallet. It was empty.

'I'll get his address from the driver,' said the barman.

'Oh no,' said Paul nervously. 'I have it.'

He took his folded ten shilling note and the florin out of his wallet and handed them over.

'Twelve shillings? Oh well, that'll do I suppose,' said the barman, taking the money.

'Good lad, Paul,' enthused the guard. 'I like your honesty.' He threw grandfather over his shoulder and Paul followed him outside.

The guard put grandfather in the front seat. He was very drunk and kept rambling incoherently.

'Any luck and he'll sleep for the whole journey,' said the guard. 'He should cause you no bother.'

Mr McKenna said nothing.

'Be seeing you,' said the guard and slammed the door.

Paul opened the back door and climbed in. As he sat down Mr McKenna sniffed the air.

'Excuse me, Paul,' said Mr McKenna, 'would you like to sit on a newspaper?'

Paul realised he had been found out and blushed.

'Yes, Mr McKenna,' he said quietly. 'I'm sorry.'

26

Mr McKenna fetched a newspaper from the boot and handed it to Paul through the open window. It was an old, yellowed copy of the *Irish Independent*. Paul saw that the headline read 'Massacre at Katanga'.

The paper below him rustled like dry leaves as they pulled away and the pleasant smell of hot leather soon gave way to that of his pee. Mr McKenna was silent.

After driving for several miles, grandfather woke up suddenly and vomited down his front. It came out in a little trickle, brown and lumpy.

'Are you alright?' Mr McKenna asked nervously. 'Shall I stop?' He pulled a cloth from under the dashboard and handed it across.

'I don't want your fucking dish-rag,' grandfather roared and slapped Mr McKenna's hand aside.

Watching in the rear-view mirror, Paul saw all the colour drain from Mr McKenna's face. He coughed nervously and returned the cloth.

Grandfather took half a bottle of brandy out of his pocket. It was Three Barrels. Paul supposed he had stolen it before he had fallen behind the bar. As grandfather uncorked the top and put it to his lips, Mr McKenna squirmed in his seat.

'Mr O'Berne . . . ' he began hesitantly.

'Fuck off!'

Mr McKenna coughed again and gripped the steering wheel so tightly that his knuckles went white. At the same time, Paul noticed, the speedometer crept above thirty.

At last the car turned up the avenue and the house sprung into view. It was a white house with a dark blue slate roof and red-painted doors and windows. Paul's heart began to beat faster. Granny would have already heard the car he thought and she would be hurrying to meet them. Before long he would be in her arms and the nightmare would be over.

The car turned from the avenue and started to edge through the piers that led into the front yard. Paul put his head out.

'You're fine Mr McKenna,' he said and looked up.

At one of the bedroom windows he caught a glimpse of granny looking down. She had a strange, set expression on her face which he had never seen before.

Mr McKenna drew up in front of the house and turned off the ignition. Grandfather was asleep and Mr McKenna got out quietly. Paul did not move but watched from the car. As Mr McKenna reached for the bell, granny's shadow appeared behind the frosted glass of the front door. Mr McKenna stepped back. Through the glass Paul saw granny struggling to pull back the door. The lintel had swollen in the snow the winter before and it was inclined to stick. Granny called out and Mr McKenna pushed from outside. The door opened and granny came out onto the step and she and Mr McKenna put their heads together. For a moment they were like hens. When granny turned towards the car, Paul jumped out and ran towards her. He wanted her to take him in her arms and clasp him to her bosom.

'Granny,' he called.

But as he ran towards her, he saw that she was not looking at him. She was staring at the front passenger seat where grandfather lay slumped. He was so low in his seat that only his white, wiry hair showed above the dashboard.

Paul stepped in front of granny and held out his arms.

'Paul,' she shouted, 'Get out of my way!'

He was dumbfounded. Her hair trailing behind, she swept past him and ran to the car.

'Granny,' he wailed.

Paul stepped aside and granny reached for the chrome door handle. As the door swung back, grandfather tumbled out like a rag doll and his bottle of Three Barrels fell to the ground and smashed.

'Oh my God,' said Granny.

'I'm very sorry,' Mr McKenna apologised.

The vomit on grandfather's front had turned dark in the heat and there was a bluebottle buzzing in the car. His trembling eyelids were fractionally apart and the whites of his eyes were visible. To Paul it looked as if he was dead.

'Mr McKenna, can you help me?' called granny.

Treading on the broken glass, she gathered grandfather back into the car.

'Will you carry him inside the house and then go for the doctor?' she asked.

Mr McKenna nodded. Granny stepped back to allow him through and Paul saw his chance.

'Granny,' he said, stepping forward and taking her arm. She would surely comfort him now, he though.

'You little brat,' she shouted, shaking her arm free from his grasp. 'You bad, bold untrustworthy boy.'

Then her face seemed to shrivel up for Paul and she struck him across the head.

He turned round, ran through the front door and bolted up the stairs. When he reached his bedroom, he tried to lock the door after himself but it was broken and the key snapped as he turned it and the ring end came away in his hand. He scurried across the linoleum and dived under the bed. In the darkness underneath, he at last felt safe and it was then he noticed his face was stinging. From his left eye down to his chin was numb and he could hear a ringing sound in his ears.

With his thumb in mouth and his head leant against the candle-wick bedspread that hung down, he cried himself to sleep. Some time later, he was woken by a voice.

'Darling. Darling pet,' the voice murmured. 'Wake up. I have some lemonade for you.'

He remembered his mother and opened his eyes and saw it was his granny. With one hand she was lifting up the bedspread and with the other she was holding out the lemonade. Because of the position in which she was crouched, he saw she was wearing pink bloomers. He stirred and felt that the cloth of his trousers where he had wet them was dried hard and was stiff.

'Come on lovey. Come out,' she coaxed.

Half-asleep, he crawled out and slipped into her arms.

'I'm sorry pet,' she said as he rested his head on her shoulder. Her hair smelt of lanolin.

'Your granny's going to be good to you from now on. You won't have to hide under the bed any more.'

Granny brought him downstairs and washed him in warm rain-water. He was happy to be treated like a baby and abetted her by keeping up the appearance of being half-asleep. She dressed him in clean clothes warmed on the Aga and boiled him two eggs. The first had a spot of blood in it which she said was lucky. As he ate them, she watched him in silence, a strange pleading expression on her face.

At nine the doctor called. It was his second visit of the day. Whilst he and granny whispered about grandfather in the passage, Paul took a piece of honeycomb and went out onto the concrete flag behind the house. It was a still summer's evening. The sky above the distant hills was streaked red and the clouds were a deep purple colour. A bullock was drinking at the trough nearby, slurping water with his big, hairy tongue. The whole world was about to go to sleep.

As he stared across the fields towards the village perched on the hill, he recalled what had happened but without much emotion. He felt just commonly unhappy, rather than abjectly miserable. It was partly that his ability to forget and unknow was already beginning to operate and it was partly that he was no stranger to human ugliness and contrariness. He had already started the retreat from life back into himself, by which the passage to adulthood is achieved.

'Come and say hello to Doctor Slattery,' his granny called from the kitchen door.

Obediently he turned and headed for the house, picking waxy bits of honeycomb from his teeth as he went.

After the doctor left, he went to bed and fell asleep almost immediately. In the middle of the night he was awoken by the sound of granny crying in the next bed.

'What's the matter, granny?' he whispered in the darkness.

'My heart is broken. Go back to sleep,' she said.

And he did.

Chapter Two

Paul sat at the kitchen table under the valve wireless. Granny beside him opened the toffee tin where she stored her make-up.

'Your poor granny is getting old,' she said.

She examined her face in the mirror balanced in front of her, pulling at her flesh so the lines disappeared.

'How old is Auntie Bridget?' he asked. 'Is she as old as grandfather?'

She patted on face-powder with an applicator shiny from use. The excess powder hovered around her in the sunlight.

'Auntie Bridget? No. She's younger.'

'Much younger?'

The powder went away and out came a scratched lipstick cartridge. She dabbed red on each cheek and then rubbed the colour in with deft circles of her fingers.

'No. Bridget's a couple of years younger.'

'Grandfather is fifty-six ... ' said Paul quietly. 'Fifty-six take away two ... Bridget's fifty-four!' he announced triumphantly.

'Paul. Enough of that. And no mention of it this afternoon, you mind.'

'All right.'

She ran the lipstick around her lips. The smell reminded him of confectionery.

'Have you got your hanky?'

Paul felt in his pocket.

'I have,' he said.

Face powder lay on the corner of the table like snow. With his right index finger he wrote his name, Paul Weismann underlined and with a full stop.

'How did they make the holes?' he asked.

She was threading the wire of an earring through an ear-lobe.

'Oh I didn't look. I think they had a machine.'

'What kind of a machine?'

'Did you ever hear about the boy who got into trouble for asking too many questions?'

'There never was such a boy, and can I have some too?'

He held out his wrist and granny up-ended the bottle she had just opened. There was a small prick of cold against his skin. He lifted his wrist to his nose. The peculiar sensation of the scent reminded him of his mother.

'Now go and say goodbye to your grandfather.'

He made a face.

'Paul. I want your help this afternoon. Not your hindrance.'

He got up and ambled towards the door. Other associations, ones from more recent times, were mingling with faraway mother. He thought of Sunday mornings; the way granny made her face up for Mass; the walk to church with her in polished shoes that pinched; the priest mumbling in Latin; the interminable service which he did not understand because of his father's insistence that he receive no religious instruction of any kind; the clink-clink as coppers were put in the collection dish; the way granny slipped him money of his own to put there; the leaving of the church and momentary blindness as he stepped from semi-darkness into light; the men of the village lolling outside against the wall; the greetings – 'Good morning Mrs O'Berne. How are you Paul?'; the unvarying Sunday lunch of chicken and lumpy white sauce; the parsley that he cut with scissors and sprinkled on the boiled potatoes; the nap that grandfather took afterwards on the sofa in the breakfast room; and the pall of depression that descended on those Sunday afternoons. . . .

He stepped into the hall. There were brown and yellow tiles on the floor and a mahogany table in the corner. One of the legs was slightly shorter than the others and rested on the base of a mouse trap.

He began to climb the stairs. How he detested what he was about to do. The black-painted bannister was cold and slightly sticky. On the wall opposite hung a series of framed photographs which granny had brought back from New York. These showed a blond girl with bobbed hair in various American settings; in a canyon; by a river; on a mountainside. At the top he stopped and looked at his favourite. This showed the girl and her horse standing in a field of white flowers.

'Don't take all day,' granny called from the kitchen.

He climbed the remaining steps to grandfather's bedroom door and knocked timidly.

'Yes. Come in,' answered Mrs McKenna inside. Mrs McKenna was minding grandfather for the afternoon.

The door opened and he saw grandfather dozing in his bed, his

32

thin body like a rake under the bedclothes. Beside the bed there was a small table covered with bottles of coloured medicine. The speckled blind was pulled down tightly and the shadow of the window frame fell darkly across its back in the shape of a cross.

'Hello Paul,' said Mrs McKenna warmly. She was knitting at the end of the bed. 'And how are you today?'

'Very well thank you.'

'And have you got a kiss for me?'

Before Mrs McKenna had arrived, he had been told not to stare at her bald patch. But as he bent forward he was not able to stop himself. He saw that she had tried to cover it with the thin hair which grew around the edges and that her scalp was the colour of the ivory keys on the piano in the London house.

Grandfather woke up with a murmur. 'Who is it?' he asked.

'It's Paul,' answered Mrs McKenna. 'He's come to say goodbye.'

'. . . Come here,' said grandfather. 'I have something for you.'

He beckoned Paul with his left hand. The last two fingers were curled back and formed a tight shape like a tropical nut. He had caught his hand in a threshing machine as a boy and they had set crooked. The two remaining fingers, as they stuck out, formed a natural 'V'. They were like a fork.

Paul stepped over and looked down. His grandfather's face was pale and there was white bristle on his chin. His wiry hair had defeated all attempts to comb it flat and stood up like the fuzz on a coconut. His eyelids were trembling.

'How are you, grandfather?'

His feet were touching the chamber pot half-full with brackish urine. Grandfather nodded and waved ambiguously.

'Under my pillow,' he whispered.

Paul tugged and pulled out a handkerchief.

'Open it,' ordered grandfather.

It was filthy with dried phlegm and blood stains. It made him feel sick. In the middle lay a sixpence. He picked it up gingerly, fearing it was wet with mucus.

'Thank you,' he said.

Grandfather shook his head. 'You've been a very good boy. I want you to know that I know that,' he said.

'Do you want anything?'

From the chamber pot the rank smell of pee drifted up. Mrs McKenna's knitting needles clacked quietly.

'No,' replied grandfather and closed his eyes.

'I think he's tired,' said Mrs McKenna.

33

'I'll go then.'

He fled down the stairs and threw open the kitchen door. Granny was standing at the table. She had already put on her black jacket. The after-sound and the after-smell of the sick-room vanished. She poured milk into a jug, set a saucer on top to keep out the dust and placed it in position on the afternoon tea-tray.

'Have you got your hanky?'

'You asked me already.' He felt his pocket. 'Yes,' he said.

'Good boy,' she replied picking up her handbag.

At the kitchen door, she dipped her finger into the porcelain font of holy water nailed to the frame. Knowing it was expected of him, Paul reached up after her. His fingers found the sponge inside the bowl tentatively. He was frightened it was a worm or, worse, a dead, mouldering mouse.

They stepped outside. The holy water on his forehead went cold. There was a strong breeze scudding clouds across the sky and ruffling the leaves of the copper beeches. Thinking vaguely of Philomena he jumped down the two steps from the back door to the flag.

'Rover! Lassie!' he called.

The dogs emerged from the hollows where they sheltered under the hedge and came to him. As he ran his fingers over their thick brown fur, they tried to catch his hands between their teeth and lick him with their vaguely foul-smelling tongues.

'Come on Paul. Don't tarry.' He straightened up and ran after his granny, the wind blowing against his face and into his ears. The dogs followed, leaping and wriggling like fish above water. They reached the gate.

'Shoo! Go away!' shouted granny, stamping her foot on the ground.

They were frightened of her and put their tails between their legs and crept away. A gust of wind blew, ruffling their fur, and for a moment they were lions with manes. They went back to their spot, licked their empty bowls with their big red tongues and settled in their hollows. These were perfectly shaped to their bodies and lined with their fur which had stuck on the sharp hedge branches over the years. Rover's nest was the darker coloured as he was the darker dog.

Granny closed the latch gate behind them and dropped down the makeshift hoop of wire that held it in place. They crossed the top of the lawn, as the front field was called, and turned down the Avenue towards the main road. It was a custom in the Red House always to leave by the back gate.

Half way down the avenue Paul spoke.

'Granny,' he blurted, 'my pee-pee's hurting.'

'What did you say, pet?'

'There's something on my pee-pee.'

She led him behind a huge bramble bush as big as a haystack, and he lowered his trousers and underpants. Scattered over his testicles were half-a-dozen or so black ticks. The tender, wrinkled prune-skin was red and inflamed around them.

'Oh lovey. How long have they been there?' she asked.

'I don't remember.'

She knelt down and nipped one at the root between her ragged finger nails. The tick came out and blood smeared over her fingertips.

Standing there whilst she removed the others, Paul could feel the long grass brushing against the back of his legs. He felt ashamed and at the same time it was pleasurable in an odd way, to be touched in that secret place. He stared into the distance. On the hill above the village he saw the parish church with its stump of a spire and the road that snaked beside it. A solitary tractor was winding its way slowly down. That summer, embarrassing hairs had begun to appear. Was this the moment to mention them? he wondered.

'All done,' said granny, pulling up his trousers, and he saw the opportunity had passed.

He buttoned himself up whilst granny cleaned her hands on a dock leaf. They walked on in silence.

At the bottom granny tried to open the gate but gave up. There was a knack to it which required lifting and pulling at the same time.

"I can never get it right,' she said as Paul clanged the gate shut behind them. 'You are a clever boy.'

He glanced across the road at the gate-keeper's lodge which stood opposite their gates rather than within the demesne grounds.

'Old Andy isn't around,' he said, referring to the decrepit old man who lived in the lodge. 'He must be sleeping.'

'When you're old, your bones require a lot of rest,' she said.

He followed her along the narrow footpath feeling mildly disappointed. If old Andy had been standing at his gate, smoking his funny pipe with its silver cap, old Andy would have dug his hand into one of his filthy pockets and brought out a shining coin for him. He preferred Andy's money to his grandfather's any day.

It took two hours to walk the road from their own house down to Bridget's, but it was an easy journey and the road wound down for the last part.

'You'll be on your best behaviour, won't you?' said granny as they approached the house.

'Oh yes,' said Paul.

Bridget lived in a low, grey bungalow near a lake. In the field beside her house lay the ruins of an impressive mansion which had once been hers and her late husband's. In a fit of greed years previously, they had sold their old house to the County Council. At that time large country houses such as theirs had had little value. The Council had knocked it down and used the stones for their local road building programme. After the war, Dutchmen and Germans had flooded into the area to establish businesses and it had come as a bitter blow to them and particularly to Bridget to discover they could have made much more money if they had kept their house and sold it to one of the foreigners.

Paul opened the front gate and they went down the concrete path. There were flower beds on either side, sparsely planted with roses. Suddenly the white front door swung open and Bridget stepped out.

'I saw you coming,' she said excitedly and ran forward. 'I've been watching the gate this last hour.

Granny and Bridget brushed cheeks and said how well each other looked.

Paul hung back shyly.

'And how's the little man?' asked Bridget bending down towards him. 'And hasn't he grown?'

'Say hullo,' said granny.

'Hullo Auntie Bridget.'

'My favourite great-nephew, you are most welcome,' she said.

As she withdrew her lips from his cheek he felt his skin was sticky.

'I've baked a cake for you,' she said, taking him by the hand and leading him towards the door. 'It's a sponge cake with strawberry jam.'

He wiped his cheek and red lipstick came away on his fingers.

The hallway was bare except for a table. A large Holy Bible rested on top, shiny black with gold-edged pages, and close beside it lay a pile of cheap religious books. At either end stood silver candlesticks, the small red candles too small for the holders held in with twists of paper.

Bridget opened the door of the parlour and motioned them to step in.

'Make yourself comfortable,' she said.

Four chairs with plain, dark, loose-fitting covers were grouped around the brown-tiled hearth. A turf fire smoked in the grate. The room smelt damp and there were yellow patches in one corner.

Bridget pulled her skirt tight around her legs and sat down.

'I'm going to fetch your tea in a moment,' she said. 'But first I just want to look at you. I haven't seen you for so long. How long is it? I haven't seen you since the funeral have I?'

'No,' replied granny.

Involuntarily, the terrible occasion sprang into Paul's mind. He stared down at the grey rug.

'You don't mind us talking about it, do you Paul?'

He realised he was being addressed. He looked up. 'No,' he said quietly.

'I believe it's terribly important to talk about it,' Bridget continued emphatically. 'It's terribly important not to keep everything bottled up inside. That was the first thing Father John said to me after James died and I've never forgotten it. It was invaluable advice.'

Paul felt his mind was emptying and that the walls of the room were moving away from him. It was like being in a dream. It was always like this before the onset of grief.

'It was such a sad occasion, wasn't it?' continued Bridget. 'Do you remember the funeral, Paul?'

He nodded.

'It was a bitter blow to lose your mother like that. But there is one consolation. At least you knew her and you have her memory to treasure for the rest of your life. Isn't that right?'

He felt the old, familiar ache tugging inside. The feeling started as a rawness at the back of his throat and seeped down to his abdomen.

'My brother – your grandfather – and I, we never knew our parents you know. They died when we were babies.' Bridget addressed him in low confidential tones. 'I remember we often used to talk about our mummy and daddy when we were children. We used to say "If only we had known them; everything would be different!"'

Bridget turned away from him and began to stare at his granny. Her expression was curious. 'Does he ... does he know it could have been S - U - I - C - I - D - E?' she said quietly, spelling the last word.

Granny shook her head emphatically and raised a finger to her lips.

The word that had been spelt out was beyond him but he could guess at what they were talking about. For reasons that were unfathomable his mother had left him alone on the earth. His eyes filled with tears.

'Oh look at the little fellow,' said Bridget. 'All this talk has made him sad.' She leaned forward and patted him on the knee. 'Do you miss your mother, darling?'

He nodded and felt a hot tear trickling down his cheek. Miss was not the word but how was he to express himself? Her absence was like a gaping hole that went on for ever and ever.

'We're going to have a nice tea,' said Bridget soothingly. 'Nice sandwiches and scones and a sponge cake,. You like sponge cake, don't you? A little bird told me sponge cake was your favourite!'

'Yes,' he said.

Granny stroked him on the back of his neck 'I haven't seen that before,' she said and pointed at the framed black and white photograph on the mantlepiece.

'Oh that old thing!' Bridget laughed. 'I found it the other day.'

She handed the photograph across. In the picture she was eighteen years old and radiant-looking. On her head she wore a woollen toque with a sprig of berries stuck in the headband. Paul glanced shyly from the photograph to Bridget. She caught his glance.

'Looking at me now Paul,' she asked, 'how old would you say I am?'

The women gave each other a knowing wink.

'I don't know.'

'Have a guess?'

Paul put on a serious face and counted five, which would be a decent pause, he thought.

'I'd say about forty.'

Bridget roared with laughter.

'Forty! My goodness Mrs O. you have this little fellow well trained. Doesn't he say the nicest things?'

She brought her face embarrassingly close to his.

'You can come to tea every day, Paul.'

'Thank you, Auntie Bridget.'

She moved her tongue with excitement between the corners of her mouth.

38

'Now what I want to know next is, do you have a girl-friend?'
'No,' he replied.
'Yes you have,' said granny.
'Who is it? Tell me who the lucky lady is', pressed Bridget.
'Philomena.' He pronounced her name so low it was nearly inaudible.
'Philomena! And have you kissed her yet?'
'No.'
As he pronounced the word, Paul remembered everything: copper beeches; Philomena's white underclothes; the herd of bullocks that had sauntered by and frightened them. . . .
'He's blushing! I think he has kissed her.' Bridget rubbed her hands with excitement. 'But we won't pry any more. A man's got to have his secrets.'
Paul lowered his reddened face. He hated thinking about that time when there were adults nearby. What if they read his thoughts – he would be discovered.
Bridget returned the photograph to the mantelpiece.
'Did you see that?' she asked pointing to a framed piece of tin hanging above the sideboard stamped with the words 'New Jersey Insurance Company'.
'My first job in the States was with them. Stenographer; ten dollars a week. Do you remember Mrs O'Berne? I found that old thing along with the photograph.'
Granny and Bridget started to talk about their times in New York together and Paul sunk into a sort of trance. He remembered his mother's smell which had been something like milk; the particular shape of her shoulders; the feel of her hair. . . . All at once he was filled with a sense of her. She was both around him and within him. Then Bridget cackled loudly and the reverie vanished.
He stared through the window at the ruins of Bridget's old mansion in the field outside. All that remained were the foundation stones overgrown with grass, an ass and three cows grazing amongst them. In the distance the lake was grey and still, except for little flurries of white at the edges. In the shallow inlets, acres of dun bullrushes swayed with the wind. He looked out to the island in the middle. He had visited there once. His mother and father had taken him over for his birthday. The island had teemed with rabbits, he remembered. They had run around in front of him without fear. They had never been hunted. The boatman had led them to the Round Tower in the middle. It had a doorway set thirty feet above the ground. The boatman had told him that when the heathens

39

came marauding, the monks on the island would retreat into the tower, pulling the ladder to the door up after themselves. 'The Christians had more noddle than the heathens,' the boatman had said.

'Come and bang the gong, Paul,' Bridget called from the kitchen door.

He crossed the room touching the backs of his thighs. They were itchy from the coarse armchair cover.

The kitchen was poky and spotless, with lineoleum on the floor worn through to the concrete around the sink and the cooker. Their tea was already laid out on a trolley and the sandwiches and the cakes were covered with a tea towel printed with the recipe for Irish coffee.

Bridget lit the cooker with a strange sparking contraption and lifted the kettle on.

'It won't be long,' she said. 'Kettle's still warm.'

'What is it?' he asked, pointing at the contraption.

'It's for lighting the gas.'

She handed it to him. It dimly resembled a potato peeler. He squeezed; a wheel whirred across a flint and sparks flew out the end.

'Very dangerous,' remarked Bridget, taking it back. She put it on the shelf beside the Perpetual Light.

'Does it ever run out?'

He pointed at the dull, red bulb that was identical to the one at home.

'You're full of questions this afternoon. No, it'll never run out.'

'Why not?'

'Because it's a perpetual light in memory of our Lord, Jesus Christ. It has to be kept burning permanently as a mark of our faith.'

He nodded automatically.

'Now get ready to bang the gong.' She scalded the teapot.

The gong stood in the corner underneath a ragged St Bridget's Cross. It was the only piece of furniture that remained from the demolished mansion. The auctioneer had forgotten to list it in the catalogue when everything else had been sold off. The frame of dark wood was carved with figures; there were dragons with wings, snarling tigers and snakes holding their tails in their mouths. The

40

hammer hung from the figure of a young man with a staff who was carrying an old man on his shoulders. The hammer's end was bulbous and spotted like a leopard's skin.

'I'll tell you when,' Bridget called as she spooned in the tea.

He glanced out of the back door. A concrete path stretched down the garden, neat beds on either side planted with cabbages and potatoes. At the bottom stood a grey bird-table and a scarecrow in an old coat.

'Off you go Paul.'

He hit the gong. His testing blow produced hardly any sound. He swung the hammer back and struck much, much harder. The face of the gong shivered and, for a moment, the small, dismal kitchen was filled with the sound.

'Bravo!' shouted Bridget. She wheeled the creaking trolley towards the door. Paul hung the hammer back where he had found it and followed her out.

He returned to his seat.

'Here you are Paul,' said Bridget.

He took the proffered side-plate from her and rested it on his thighs. It was cold. He contemplated the sandwiches on the trolley. They were made of white shop-bread cut very thin. Half the fillings were pale green and the remainder were reddy-pink.

'Cucumber and salmon,' said Bridget, pointing out to him which were which.

He took a sandwich with a red streak down the middle and bit into it. It was an odd taste, a burnt taste and slightly dry. In the middle there was a piece of round bone, a salmon vertebra. It was like wax honeycomb to him, only it crumbled more readily.

'I was just thinking in the kitchen,' said Bridget, 'how I miss the States. I'd give my right arm to go back over before I die. Not to live there, you understand – just to see it. But I imagine it's changed since my day. I probably wouldn't recognise it.'

'Oh yes, it's a concrete jungle now,' agreed granny. 'The coloureds you know.'

Granny held out the platter to Paul.

'Have another,' she said.

He put a cucumber sandwich on his plate.

'Do you remember, Paul,' asked Bridget, 'when you came here as a baby?'

She began to pour the tea through a sieve.

He shook his head.

'You were very small, just walking, and we were all drinking tea.

41

But you were too little to have a cup so you weren't given one, and you started crying! Are you sure you don't remember this?'

'No,' he replied and looked down at the sandwich on his plate. He was longing to take a bite but he knew it would be impolite to do so until she finished.

'Well, anyway, you bawled and you bawled and you bawled and in the end the only way to stop you was to put some tea in a saucer for you with sugar and a lot of milk. Your mammy held it, God bless her, and you drank that. You were as happy as a sandboy then! But now you're a big boy and so you shall have your own cup and saucer today.'

'Thank you.'

He took his tea from her and bit into his sandwich. His first impression was of something cold, salty and bland. He gripped one of the green slices between his teeth and began to investigate it with his tongue. It felt slithery and it reminded him of mucus. A wave of nausea overwhelmed him. He made a face and a whining noise.

'What's the matter lovey?' asked his granny.

'I don't like it!' he mumbled.

'He doesn't like it,' explained granny apologetically. 'He's never had cucumber before.

'Go out the kitchen door,' said Bridget slightly crossly, 'and you'll see a bucket on your right. Put it in there.'

He got up and ran through to the kitchen. He was out of sight there and he spat the cucumber sandwich into his palm.

'Can I look at the scarecrow?' he called from the back door. They did not have one at home. They scared their birds by hanging up rows of tin cans which clanked in the wind.

'Don't be long or your tea'll get cold.'

He opened the door and saw the bucket. It was rivetted down the side and the handle was made of rope. He scraped the sandwich off his palm. In the bucket there was a black banana skin, a John West's salmon tin and an empty salmon paste jar. Bridget had supplemented the salmon with paste, he guessed. That explained the strange taste.

Wiping his hands on his trousers, he made his way down to the scarecrow. The body was a simple cross of wood, with a grey ladies' coat draped over it, tightly belted at the waist. The head was an elongated Libbys Grapefruit Juice tin, with holes gouged in it to represent the eyes, nose and mouth. The pockets were bulging. Without thinking, he reached into one. It felt dry and crinkling inside and when he pulled out his hand he saw he was holding a

42

handful of leaves. A squeeze of the other pocket revealed it contained the same.

He turned and retraced his steps.

As he re-entered the parlour, granny and Bridget fell silent.

'Have some cake,' said Bridget handing him a portion of sponge cake. He took the plate and sat down. The women looked at one another and granny nodded her head. It was intended to be imperceptible but he saw it.

'Is he very B-A-D then?' Bridget spoke quietly and the crucial word 'bad' she spelt, repeating the technique she had used once already.

Paul stared at his plate. The strawberry jam between the sponge was brownish with woody pips.

'He's on the mend,' said granny wearily. 'He's a strong man.'

'Oh yes,' replied Bridget, 'he'll outlive us all – I've always said that! – despite the drink, despite everything!'

There was a silence gaping like a cave. Paul heard the sound of his own chewing. The turf fire spluttered and wind sighed in the yew trees that grew along the back of the house. The sky began to darken.

'It must be a terrible burden for you to bear.'

Granny shrugged.

'It's not that. . . .' Her voice died away.

Paul wet the tip of his finger and started to pick up the sugar granules scattered across his plate.

Granny continued quietly: 'He put a B-E-T on the horse and you know what happened. Well what he put on was the L-O-A-N from the bank.'

'Oh my God!'

'We B-O-R-R-O-W-E-D it. It was to hire men to bring in the harvest. Unless we find it, we'll have to go. We'll be O-U-T on the roads.'

'My God! It there no end to the mischief of that man? He's my own brother and I shouldn't say this, but that was a wicked thing to do.'

Bridget took her glasses off and put them on again and looked across at Paul.

'Paul! Your plate is empty.' She cut another slice of sponge and passed it across on a serving knife with a decorated blade.

'It's a bad business,' she added.

The room went quiet again. Paul stared at his cake and listened. He heard the creaking of wood as Bridget turned in her chair. He

43

lifted his eyes slowly. Bridget was in profile, heaping turf on to the hearth. Her nose was bony; her chin jutted out; and her cheeks were purple with little worms of red in them. As she straightened up and sat back, clenching her copper rheumatism bracelet tight around her wrist, he noticed granny was watching her with an expression which was sad and expectant at the same time. He lowered his eyes again.

At last Bridget spoke, 'It's not a very nice state of affairs, I must say. Especially as you have added responsibilities.'

Bridget was staring at him. Paul could feel it. He remained motionless. One gesture and they would know he was understanding everything and he would have to leave.

'I don't know what to do,' pleaded granny. 'I can't see any way out of it.'

'Well you know, I can't do anything to help you. Between the taxes and the rates and the new guttering and every other expense on top of that, I haven't got two brass farthings to rub together.'

'Paul?' snapped his grandmother abruptly. 'Have you had enough to eat?'

He looked up shyly.

'Here,' she said, handing him two halves of a buttered scone. 'Go outside and play now.'

He rose from his seat in haste, anxious to appear obliging, and inadvertently banged his elbow against his saucer and the full tea cup which were balanced on the wide, rounded armrest. They fell onto the rug almost soundlessly. The thin porcelain cup cracked in two and the milky tea formed a puddle in which there floated a few swollen tea-leaves like tadpoles.

'Oh Paul.' Granny's voice was quiet.

'Oh you clumsy little boy.' His aunt's voice was loud and cutting. She quickly got to her feet and bent over the broken cup.

'I didn't mean to do it,' he said. His Adam's apple was bobbing up and down. 'I'm sorry, Auntie Bridget.' The scone he was holding began to break up from the heat and the perspiration of his palm.

'Yes I know that but you must look what you're doing in future and be more careful.'

Granny stood beside Bridget peering over her shoulder. 'Paul, go and get the floor cloth,' she ordered.

He ran into the kitchen, put his scone on the side and grabbed the blue cloth hanging over the side of the sink.

When he returned to the parlour Bridget was at the sideboard rummaging through a drawer.

44

'I know it's here. It's here somewhere,' she muttered.

'Give me that' exclaimed granny. She took the floor cloth from him and bent down. After a few brisk rubs, the pile of the rug stood up in clumps restored almost to its natural colour. With a deft movement she picked up the tea-leaves in the folds of the cloth.

Paul did not feel right where he was standing and yet he was not able either to sit down or go out.

'Can I do anything to help?' he asked.

Bridget did not reply.

He stared at her back with its slight hump just below her neck. Had she heard him? Or was she pretending not to?

In the kitchen, granny banged open the back door and dropped his discarded scone in the bucket.

'I've found it,' cried Bridget. She ran into the kitchen carrying a tube and the two halves of the cup.

Paul stood and watched through the doorway. His granny spread newspaper on the table. Bridget sat down and pushed her glasses up her nose. The thick lenses magnified her eyes to an abnormal size and he saw her face as only eyes and nothing else. She smeared glue from the tube along the ragged edges and pressed the broken halves together, then wiped away the excess with a matchstick.

'Paul, could you bring the rubber bands?' she called. 'They're on the sideboard.'

He stepped across to the dark piece of furniture. It was solid and Victorian with spiralling pillars at either end and a long low mirror running along the back. What did Bridget mean? His heart was beating. He wanted to oblige but where was he to look? He peered into the drawer that was hanging out. Letters from the bank, brucellosis testing cards, a large bottle of pills with an illegible prescription stuck to the front, several back issues of *The Farmer* magazine, a silver scissors, needles and thread, a *Bloodstock Breeding Catalogue* for 1938, a cardboard box that had once contained shotgun cartridges and a great deal of other not immediately recognisable clutter lay in front of him. But the rubber bands were nowhere in sight.

'In the silver jug,' called Bridget in answer to his prayer.

He peered inside the little silver one on the tray. Saved! He tipped the different coloured rubber bands onto his palm and carried them like a heap of worms to the kitchen.

Bridget fixed a thick yellow one around the rim and a brown band around the base.

'Will it be all right?' he asked.

45

'It'll always have a crack but at least I can display it. The set won't go short,' she replied.

'Well that's something I suppose,' remarked granny.

He looked down at the focus of disaster. It was a white cup with a yellow and black pattern and a delicate handle. The crack snaked down the side, dark brown glue oozing out of it.

'Would you like me to do the washing up?' he asked.

'Oh no. I think you've broken quite enough for today.'

'Why don't you go out and play,' suggested his granny.

Bridget was noisily folding up pieces of newspaper. He glimpsed a photograph of a young girl in a dress. 'I think it's raining,' she said.

Granny lifted a net curtain from the kitchen window. Outside a damp drizzle was slowly falling from a dismal sky. He imagined the dogs; they would be dry under the hedge in their hollows whilst all around them the rain would be dripping through the hedge-leaves. How good it would be he thought, to be there with them, curled up against their warm bodies. . . .

'Go and sit inside,' said his granny.

He went back to the parlour and resumed his seat. In the kitchen there was much banging and clattering and the kettle was put back on the stove.

A quiet burr of conversation drifted out. He began to listen, fearful that he might be the subject of their talk. When he realised they were discussing grandfather, grandfather's convalescence and Mrs McKenna, a great wave of relief swept over him.

The two women returned, Bridget bearing the teapot on a tray.

'Would you like some more tea Paul?' she asked.

'Yes,' he said although he did not. He assented out of politeness and his fear of crossing her.

She poured a great deal of milk and then a little tea into the stout, dull-white cup that she had brought.

'I'm going to give you a different cup this time,' she said, handing it across. It was thick and chipped. 'It won't matter a jot if you break it.'

He balanced the cup and saucer on his lap and stared down at the wet stain on the rug. The women began to speak. He sipped at his tepid tea. Outside the window rain was falling in sheets made up of silvery-grey needles. The donkey and the three cows were gone. The field stretched, empty and wet to the lake, which in turn stretched empty and grey to the island. He imagined the rabbits there cowering under the prickly gorse bushes. Water trickled down the chimney and the fire hissed. . . .

'Look! It's breaking,' exclaimed Bridget.

All three turned and gazed out the window. On the distant horizon a small patch of delicate, pale blue sky appeared and a moment later the sun began to shine. The room was filled with brilliant sunshine. He ran his tongue around his teeth, furry from the milky tea.

'And look at that,' continued Bridget.

The three of them went to the window and looked out.

In the sky there were two huge rainbows side by side. They started somewhere above the bungalow and stretched to the edge of the lake. Paul tried to make out the seven colours which he had been told made up the rainbow but he was only able to see three: blue, green and yellow.

'Isn't God's universe a marvel!' said Bridget.

'Yes,' echoed granny.

Paul said nothing. The fields and the sky seemed to glisten. It was as if they had been washed and polished. The lake was a smooth mirror. The world was always this way after rain in the summer and it lifted the heart.

'You can go out and play now,' said his granny.

'Yes,' he replied.

He ran across wet fields, soaking his shoes and socks, and arrived out of breath. The boat-house stood in a clearing of trees, a wooden-framed building armoured with sheets of corrugated iron. From the back end stretched a small, dark canal which fed into the lake.

He pushed open the door. Inside there was a stone walkway on three sides of a pool. It had been from here that they had taken the boat when they had gone on the trip to the island. But there was no boat now. At the bottom of the pool he could see rusty tin cans and old black bottles. A cloud of small, silvery fish flashed by. He looked around. Oars and tackle, buoys and ropes hung from the walls. There was a smell of rotting canvas and creosote. Something caught his eye. It was hanging from the ceiling in a far dark corner. The black, evil pellets on the floor, acrid and bitter smelling, told him what it was even before he got close enough to see. It was a bat. Bats were frightening. They flew at night and he understood they had no eyes. Once Joseph had told him how a bat had strayed into a house – it had flown down the chimney – and had got itself caught in the tresses of a young lady. The bat had thrashed around in a frenzy like a fly in a spider's web. In the end three men had held the lady down and cut the bat free. When she woke up the next morning her hair had turned grey.

He stared up at the small, hanging creature. Was it alive or dead? It was a sack of bones in a furry skin and this somehow confirmed Joseph's story. His heart started to beat. He turned round and ran out.

Paul made a circuit of the fields and returned to the bungalow an hour or so later. He did not arrive at the back door from where he had set out but at the front. The Yale key was in the lock as it always was. He turned it silently and went in. Standing in the hall beside the table and the red candles in the silver candlesticks, he heard low voices in the parlour. He crept over to the door and inclined his head to listen.

Inside the room Bridget was speaking, 'When John died, may he rest in peace, my heart was broken. I could do nothing; I couldn't eat; I couldn't sleep; I just wanted to die. One night, when I was at my lowest, I got out of my bed upstairs and I got down on my knees. It was so silent here in the house and I could hear nothing but the ticking of my clock. I started to pray. "Dear God," I said, "grant me your forgiveness and your strength". He must have heard my plea for suddenly I felt his presence all around me. He was with me as clearly as you are now. It was the oddest sensation I have ever experienced. We communicated – not with words you understand – and suddenly everything became clear to me. I understood that John's death had a purpose in God's plan. John had lived his life and at the end of his allotted time God had taken him. Suddenly it was morning and I saw the daylight shining through the curtains. The hours had flown by without my knowing. I got dressed and I came down to make myself a cup of tea. I felt at peace with myself for the first time since John passed away. I felt strong and I knew that for the rest of my time on earth, with God's help, I would be free from the despair that had gripped me and I would find the strength to carry on. If you can find it in your heart to do the same, to pray to him and beg for his forgiveness and his help, I know everything will be all right. You will find the money; you will pay the bank. Do you understand? Have you heard what I said?'

There was a silence and then his granny said very quietly, 'You don't understand. My heart is broken.'

When Paul heard these words, he remembered how granny had cried in the night and had said the same words then. He felt ashamed. Why had he gone back to sleep instead of speaking?

48

' . . . I don't know what to do. I don't know where to turn. . . . '

She began to sob, making a noise like a low intermittent drone.

He turned away and crept out of the front door without making a sound.

What was he to do now? He crouched against the back wall beside empty Calor Gas canisters.

'One, two, three . . . ' he began counting inwardly.

He continued to a hundred. That was surely a long time? Then he went round the house and entered by the back door, banging it noisily after himself. As he stepped across the kitchen he expected to hear one of the women calling to him but neither did. He looked through the doorway into the parlour and saw granny and Bridget kneeling on newspapers on the floor. He softened his tread to a tip-toe. Bridget opened her eyes behind her glasses and wearily lifted her head. He made an apologetic grimace and stopped moving. Bridget lowered her head again and a moment later, never quite dovetailing, whispers of double prayer filled the room.

He looked at granny kneeling with her back towards him. Through her cream-coloured blouse and check-patterned skirt, he saw the bumps and ridges of her brassiere and corset. She always removed them in the dark and so he had no idea what they looked like. All he knew was the clinging rubbery sound of their being put on or taken off, sounds that he half-heard at night in darkness or in the morning in slumber. On her legs she was wearing lisle stockings with dark seams at the back that were round like a vein. Her shoes were brown as well and the soles were scuffed white with wear. The green curtains by the open window billowed and fell. The rank smell of wet grass drifted in. His thoughts turned to the copper beeches at home; the sound of the wind sighing in their branches; the purple colour of the light when one stood inside the circle; the whiteness of his cousin's skin. . . .

'Amen,' murmured granny and Bridget.

With crooked hands and fingers bowed they made the sign of the Cross. Paul's attention returned to the present.

Using the armchairs for assistance, the two women stood up, their knees creaking like corks being pulled from bottles.

'Come and sit lovey,' said granny turning towards him. She looked happy to him and as he went past, she ran her fingers through his hair.

The clock was shaped like a hump-backed bridge. There was a tinkling whirring sound and the hour began to strike. Eight chimes followed, throaty rather than bell-like. Through the windows sun-

49

shine streamed from the sinking sun, lighting the room with peculiar brightness. Shadows stretched from the tea-cups and the silver on the sideboard.

'Well, we must be going,' said granny.

'Oh no,' exclaimed Bridget.

Granny ran the tip of her lipstick cartridge around her mouth and rolled her lips.

'We must, mustn't we Paul?'

He nodded. Ever since he had blundered in on the women praying, he had felt obliged to be silent. Hours of not talking had made him morose. He was anxious to go.

Granny stood up.

'Well,' said Bridget, 'it's been wonderful. I've had more conversation this afternoon than I've had for ages. Living alone, you know, you get "lonesome" as the Yanks say.'

She put her hands to her cheeks and held them for a moment. He looked out the window towards the distant hills. They were blue in the evening light. His thoughts ran forward. . . . After he and his granny left his auntie would have dinner alone; she would eat it off the tray that was sitting on the kitchen table waiting for her; her sharp white teeth would work the food over and over until it had a soft, digestible consistency which he did not like to think about. After washing up just as carefully, she would listen to the radio or else she would read one of her religious books. The stiff cardboard backs would creak and split as she bent the books open. The paper would be coarse and the cheap print would smudge the tips of her fingers. It would get dark. She would pull on the brass knobs and the dark-green heavy curtains would swish into place. The room would be sealed off from the world. The time for bed would arrive. She would lock the back door; she would hide the key as was customary under the enamel soap-dish – everybody he knew seemed to do this – and she would turn off the lights one by one and go upstairs. Then would follow the putting on of a stiff, white night-dress, kneeling and praying on the cold linoleum at the side of the bed, climbing in between ever-so-slightly damp sheets and finally the turning out of the last light. Alone in the bungalow that was alone in the fields, Bridget would lie propped up on pillow and bolster and would wait for sleep. . . .

These images ran through Paul's mind one after the other. He had a talent for picturing events in this way which he had developed after his mother died. During these months, he had endlessly compared what he had been doing with what he would be doing had

50

she still been alive. These reveries had been bittersweet, bringing as much pain as comfort. In the end some change had occurred. He lost interest. But the ability remained.

Granny put on her black hat and began to pin it in place, dextrously weaving the needle through straw and hair.

'I'll convey you to the road,' said Bridget.

'Oh no,' replied granny 'long drawn-out farewells are always the worst.'

He rose to his feet and followed the two women into the hall.

'It's turning chilly,' Bridget took her grey cardigan from the hatstand. She threw it over her shoulders like a cape and opened the front door. A light breeze wafted in.

'I love these long evenings, don't you?'

His aunt folded her arms. The three of them stood in the doorway and looked out. Shadows lengthened across the grass.

'It'll be midsummer soon, just imagine!' said granny. 'And then the nights will start to draw in and it'll be winter before we know it.'

The mystery of summer. When the days were longest, the weather should by rights be at its hottest, he believed. But in fact it was in August and September, when the days were getting appreciably shorter and when there was already a winter nip in the air come evening, that the sun seemed to shine most brightly. It did not make sense.

'Well, the weather hasn't been too bad so far,' said Bridget.

'Yes, that's true. Let's hope it holds.'

It was time to go.

'Goodbye Bridget,' said granny.

'Goodbye Lily.'

When he heard the word, a familiar feeling like goose-pimples began to spread through his insides. 'Lily, Lily . . . ' he repeated to himself as the women kissed. It was so strange to think of the woman he knew as granny as having a name.

'Goodbye my little man,' said Bridget bending towards him. 'You'll come again very soon I hope.'

'Bye-bye,' he replied, staring up at her blue eyes huge behind her glasses. The zoo came to mind; dark rooms and neon lit tanks; reptiles and fish. . . .

'Say thank you for tea,' instructed granny.

'Thank you for the tea Auntie Bridget.'

'Good boy.' His aunt puckered his cheek.

The women kissed again. They sauntered down the path. A

church bell rang somewhere in the distance. Bridget began to recite in a monotone:

> The curfew tolls the knell of parting day,
> The lowing herd wind slowly o'er the lea,
> The ploughman homeward plods his weary way,
> And leaves the world to darkness and to me.

Granny clapped, the sound muted in the open air. 'My God!' she exclaimed, 'but you've a fantastic memory. You always had.'

'So what. . . .' Bridget shrugged and brusquely opened the gate to let them through.

'You've been so generous to us,' said granny, 'I don't know how to thank you. . . .'

'Yes, yes.'

Bridget lifted her glasses and pressed her eyes with a finger and thumb.

'I think you'd better make a start if you want to be home before dark,' she said, 'rather than lingering.'

For a moment he thought she was annoyed until he saw tears trickling down her cheeks.

'Oh Bridget,' said granny softly.

Granny reached forward and took her by the wrist. Bridget pulled herself free and turned her head aside. With her hands she made a 'shooing' movement. The message was unmistakeable.

The gate clicked shut behind them and they started to walk. The track was narrow with grass and buttercups growing in the middle.

On one short stretch a passing tractor had spattered oil and the black globules shone like wet tar. In the distance the track veered out of sight behind a huge rock.

As he trotted after his granny he felt an uncomfortable feeling in the middle of his back. Bridget was watching from her garden. He and granny were joined to her by an invisible cord that stretched and stretched and stretched. . . . Not until they were out of sight would the cord be broken and then the feeling that they were abandoning her would disappear.

They drew near to the rock. It was like the hull of an upturned boat, ridges like plimsoll lines running around it and white lichen like barnacles everywhere.

They turned to make their last farewell. Bridget was still by the gate, arms crossed, her grey cardigan hanging over her shoulders. She was a small figure in her neat garden. They waved; she waved back. They turned; she turned.

52

Rounding the rock he stole one final glance over his shoulder. Bridget was standing half-way down the garden path with her hands held to her face.

The road stretched ahead through a plantation of trees, silver birches mostly. They were light, almost white-skinned, with dark gashes on their trunks like open mouths. Behind the plantation on a low hill loomed a burnt-out mansion of brick, with wide intervals along the front which had once been doors and windows.

'Who used to live there?' He pointed at the remains.

'I've told you before.'

'Tell me again.'

'Well,' began granny, 'that was where the Wallaces lived. They were English landlords. They got burnt out in the Troubles and they went back to England.'

They were drawing closer to the ruins. The sun was slanting almost horizontally from the west. It fell flatly on the front of the building vividly lighting up the brickwork, whilst the spaces of the old doors and windows were filled with enormous black shadows.

'Tell me about the party,' said Paul.

'The Wallaces were a rich family and they gave a party each year for all the tenants; and this particular year it was a special party. It was George V's coronation. I had just started school and I had my holidays. I must have been six or seven. And we went, the whole family, because we had land off them. I carried my shoes from home and I put them on at the gate. The avenue to their house was lined with these huge trees that towered over you. . . .'

He ran his eyes along the avenue that led up to the house. The trees were gone and the stumps reminded him of a row of buttons.

' . . . My heart wouldn't stop beating as I walked up and when I got to the top I couldn't believe my eyes. There were all these trestle tables on the lawn with white tablecloths laid out with plates of food and jugs, and hanging from the trees there were paper streamers and doilies and Chinese-lanterny things with tassels. These tassels were blowing in the wind and I remember staring up at them. I couldn't keep my eyes off them. And hanging from every window of the house was the English flag, the Union Jack. It was a hot day and there were a lot of wasps. There was lemonade or something like that in the jugs and that brought them out. There was a ceilidh band with dancing and Mrs Wallace had her piano carried outside and sang songs. And then in the middle of all this company and excitement, I was reaching for this scone off a plate and wasn't there a wasp crawling around on top? And he stung me on my finger. . . .'

53

She pointed to the spot.

' . . . I was screaming and roaring and they brought me round to the back of the house and into the kitchens. It was hot in there. They had been baking pies. All the oven doors were open and the pies were laid out in rows to cool. A big cook in a white coat went and got bicarbonate of soda and he put some on my finger. I stopped crying then and I was put up on his knee and he sang to me:

> Oh Danny Boy, the pipes, the pipes are calling,
> From glen to glen and down the mountainside,
> The summer's gone and all the roses falling,
> 'Tis you, 'tis you must go and I must bide.

'And what happened then granny?'

'Oh I must have been brought back to my family. I don't remember exactly.'

'And then?'

'We played games: hop-scotch and skipping and hide-and-seek. Then night came and we went home.

They walked on in silence, absorbed in their own thoughts. The woods grew abnormally silent and quite ordinary shapes started to assume a grotesque appearance, as it grew darker. Paul moved closer to his granny and took comfort from the movement of her arm against his shoulder.

The huge wood of birch trees came to an end and the road started to twist and turn. A motor car approached, a dark shape like an animal, with shining eyes. They stepped back onto the verge and, as it passed, they stared at the driver hopefully to see if they recognised him. But it was no one they knew. They walked on.

The clear parts of the sky became like mother-of-pearl, pale and smooth, whilst the clouds turned to dark purple fringed with red. Paul remembered something odd which had happened the summer before. He had been over from England on his holidays. It had been a particularly hot night; he had been lying in bed with only a sheet covering him and the window beside him had been wide open. Suddenly the blind had lifted and three silver-edged creatures had flown in, one after the other; a blind bat, his black furry skin stretched so tightly over his thin bones it looked as though they would snap; a fox, the colour of autumn bracken, with a pointed snout and a white bushy tail; and finally a fairy, a stocky figure with a wand in each hand. At the end they had all come back together and swirled and pirouetted in front of him before finally flying away for ever. The event had always puzzled him and he wondered if he should mention it? But in the end he decided against it. There were many events like this for which there was no proper explanation and such matters, he dimly recognised, were best kept to oneself.

When they got to their demesne the stars were shining above.

'Let's link' said granny as Paul clanged the gate shut. It was an established ritual to link arms for the stones and ruts of the avenue were hazardous at night.

He slipped his arm around granny's and her hand found his. Its shape and weight were as distinctive as a well-worn shoe.

They started to walk. In Black's field as it was called at the side, unseen sheep sighed and shifted. He threw back his head. The Milky Way was dense and thick. It was like hundreds of necklaces stretching across the sky.

'Look at the stars. They're like God's candles.'

'Ah pet, is that what they are?' asked granny mildly.

'Yes.'

'And why are they there?'

'God lights them at night so everyone can find their way home.'

There was a scampering in the darkness and two shapes with swinging tails bounded towards them.

He slipped his hand from granny's and crouched down.

'Hello,' he cried excitedly.

The dogs banged against him, almost knocking him over. He felt their cold snouts on his face and smelt their strong, faintly repellent breath.

'My, my, they're over-excited!' said granny as she patted them, hesitating like a stranger would. She fed the dogs once a day but as a rule she never touched them.

The dogs thrashed around him in a frenzy for a few moments and then, as suddenly as they had arrived, they darted off into the darkness on some mysterious errand.

Paul jumped to his feet.

The cream-painted upper walls of the house glimmered in the darkness ahead of them. Away in the bushes, the dogs barked with excitement.

'I'm like your mother now,' said granny. 'You know that.'

55

Her voice was soft and coaxing; the same voice she used with her hens.

'And nothing's going to happen to you. I shall always be with you. You're safe with me.'

She put her arm around his shoulder and give him a little sideways hug in the darkness.

Paul climbed into bed and pulled out four squares of chocolate from the breast pocket of his pyjamas. His granny had given them to him when they had come in from the dark. They were thick squares from the end of a block. He decided to save two pieces for the morning and put them on the window ledge above his bed. The other two he jammed up against the roof of his mouth. He turned on his side and closed his eyes. Odd fragments from the day drifted across his mind. The freshly glued cup on Bridget's kitchen table . . . his great-aunt's magnified blue eyes staring at him as she said goodbye . . . the stars in the night sky like a basket of light. Melted chocolate was beginning to slide down his throat. A picture of Philomena floated in. He imagined himself beside her. They were in a dell with trees growing around the rim. Philomena lay down on the ground. He lay down on top of her. He held her. She held him. They started to press against each other. He slipped off his sandals; one then the other. His feet were bare. He pushed his toes against the heels of her shoes. They came off easily. She was wearing white ankle socks. He wriggled his left toe behind the elasticated top of her left sock and pulled it down, repeating the process on the other side. Their toes touched. He started to rub with his middle against her. Her dress began to rise. It rose from her knees to her waist; from her waist to her shoulders; and finally, miraculously, it rose over her head and came away from her altogether. He stopped pressing with his middle and began pressing with his chest. One by one the pearl coloured buttons of her bodice came undone and then her bodice was gone. Philomena's chest was pale and white and her belly-button was a small hole with a mysterious web of skin at the centre. He pressed downwards. Her white knickers started to move down her thighs. They slid over her knee and down to her ankles. With a deft movement of his bare feet he removed them. Suddenly he was naked too. It was now that the miracle took place. He knew it did. But how precisely was it achieved? It was always this way with these reveries of his. He would get to this stage and then he could get no further. He went back to the start again. Perhaps next time round the secret would be revealed? But at the point where the last button of Philomena's bodice came undone, he fell asleep. . . .

Chapter Three

He crept into the parlour smelling of old apples with crinkled skins and the white furniture polish which granny applied monthly. The carpet was thick like moss beneath his feet. In the gilded mirror his image glimmered palely, flanked by two dolphins, leaping figures of red and blue coloured glass. Opposite the window stood the sideboard, granny's long, dark store-house. As he pulled back the door the hinges shrieked like a whelping dog.

'What are you doing Paul?' Her ears were ever alert to noises, especially those coming from her best room.

'Nothing,' he called back.

'Don't break anything.'

'I won't.'

The shelves were packed with her most valuable comestibles: dark-blue boxes of Cadbury's chocolate; tins of grapefruit and mandarins, the labels spotted brown with age; and jars of apple, gooseberry and blackcurrant jam, all with greaseproof paper stretched tightly like drumskins across their necks.

He reached down a silver spoon and began to tap the taut surfaces, producing a noise like that of rain falling on leaves in the woods. Then he remembered why he had come, closed the door with a bang and scurried over to the tall, elegant, glass-fronted cabinet lined with cheap wallpaper. On the shelves granny kept her knick-knacks: a crockery set from a doll's house; four gold chairs and a table which were pin-cushions but which had never been used for that purpose; tiny animals made of glass including a mother kangaroo with two glass babies in her pouch; a set of amber-coloured carnival glasses decorated with bunches of grapes which she had won during her giddy days in New York; and a porcelain lady's boot with 'A present from Queenstown' written on the front. Underneath the cabinet lay a pile of paper bags, salvaged from shopping expeditions and flattened out for re-use. Lifting them away he found the abandoned mouse-trap was still there. It was a cheap contraption of light wood and springs, with the trade name 'Little Nipper' branded on the top. Granny bought her mouse-traps in the Creamery Store at sixpence for six. He had accompanied her once when she had gone to buy them and he remembered how a whole nest-like cluster had been lifted down from the rafters by means of a cunning stick.

He set the trap down on the carpet, pulled back the death-dealing bar and hooked in place the thin spit of metal which held the whole mechanism in readiness. A strip torn off a paper bag was twisted into a taper. He settled on his stomach and reached forward with it to the little point of metal to which he knew the bait was fixed.

'Ding-dong' went the electric bell as he was about to stroke it.

He lifted his head. This was incredible. No one ever came to their front door.

'Ding-dong' it sounded again.

'Paul! Answer it, would you!' called granny.

Wearily he rose to his feet and went out to the porch. He took hold of the key sticking out of the lock like a finger and pulled his hardest. Three heaves and the door swung back juddering to reveal a tall, bulky man with cropped hair and pale blue eyes.

'Good afternoon,' greeted the man in a thick accent, 'is this the house of Mr O. Berne?' He separated the O. and the Berne making the surname sound double-barrelled.

'I'm afraid he's resting at the moment.'

'Ah, I see. This is not a good time. Would it be convenient perhaps if I called back later?'

There were footsteps in the hall and then his granny appeared beside him.

'You are Mrs O. Berne?'

'I am,' she replied cautiously, brushing back the hair from her face.

'I am searching for Mr O. Berne. My name is Schmidt. I am with a large company in Hamburg and I would like to speak with your husband about some business.'

'What sort of business would that be?'

'We are building a paper factory here in Ireland and we are finding a site soon we hope.'

'He hasn't been very well recently.'

'I am sorry to hear that. Perhaps I could leave you the telephone number of the hotel where I am staying and Mr O. Berne could telephone me?'

'Well . . . no. He hasn't been very well as I said but he does get up in the afternoons now. . . .'

'You need have no fear Mrs O. Berne. Our meeting will be short

59

and to the point. I shall not tire your husband out. Let me introduce myself properly: Herman Schmidt, Hamburg Paper Company.'

Mr Schmidt stretched out a large, strong hand with a gold ring on the little finger.

'Very pleased to meet you.' She wiped her palms. 'I've been baking,' she explained.

The adults shook hands. On her cheek Paul noticed there was a small patch of flour.

'Come in, please.'

Mr Schmidt stepped forward, the metal caps on his heels clicking loudly on the tiles.

The front door slammed, sounding like the bang from a far-off quarry.

'I'm afraid the door's a bit stiff,' apologised granny. 'Paul, would you show Mr Schmidt into the front room?'

'It's this way,' said Paul opening the door.

The front room was not the best room in the house – unquestionably that was the parlour – and yet, for reasons he did not grasp, it was traditional for all guests to be received there.

Mr Schmidt swept past him and settled in the armchair by the fire-place. It was grandfather's traditional seat. He would not be pleased.

'Do you mind if I smoke?' asked Mr Schmidt, interrupting these unpleasant thoughts.

'No, please go ahead.'

He reached down the 'Sweet Afton' ashtray and put it on the arm rest. Old ashes smelt in the fire-place and a stale smell hung in the air. There was an antagonism to fresh air in the house and the windows were rarely opened.

'My God!' said Mr Schmidt suddenly, giving his forehead a smart bang with his hand. 'I have just this moment realised. You must forgive me. I have not asked your name.'

'Paul.'

'Ah Paul, that is a nice name. Paul ... ?'

'Weissman.'

'I am very pleased to meet you.'

He leaned forward and shook Paul's hand.

'Weissman ... ?' He held the pipe over his tobacco pouch, packing the bowl with dark strings of tobacco. 'You are not called O. Berne?'

'They're my grandparents.'

'And you live here with them?'

'Yes.'

'This must be very nice for you, living here. I too was bred in the countryside. On a little farm. This is why I asked my firm to send me here – to your beautiful country – so I could leave behind the dirt and the smog of the city and breathe clean air and see clean fields.'

Mr Schmidt lit his tobacco. Paul's palms were getting sticky. Wiping them on the sides of his legs he glanced surreptitiously at the gilt mirror hanging above the mantelpiece. His own face was white and anxious whilst Mr Schmidt in profile was big and burly with a thick bull-neck. He tried to make out if Mr Schmidt looked bored but his face was obscured by the smoke he was blowing out. The smell of his tobacco was honeyed and slightly sickly. He looked up at the two busts of female heads which stood on either end of the mantelpiece. One was called Iris and the other was called Gala, their names being printed underneath. Their skins were yellowing alabaster; their lips were a faint rose-red; and the most tender poignant smiles lit up their lovely faces. 'Dear Iris, dear Gala,' he prayed, 'please help me to think of something to say. . . .'

On the other side of the hall there was a click and a clatter abnormally loud-sounding because of the silence.

Mr Schmidt withdrew his pipe. 'What was that?' he asked.

'It's a mouse-trap.'

'We must go and see.'

Paul led Mr Schmidt into the parlour.

'Ah' exclaimed Mr Schmidt, peering down. 'you have caught a little princeling, I should say.'

Paul bent forward and saw a brown mouse with a tiny fragile body. The spring-loaded bar had crushed it behind the head forcing its eyeballs from their sockets. They hung down loosely by threads of crimson nerve – small, black, jellied dots. There was blood on the wooden base, dark and glutinous.

'Poor little fellow,' he said.

'What bait did you use?'

'I didn't. I just had it set up for playing.'

'No cheese?'

'No cheese!'

'This was not a "mouse-of-the-world" to be caught by a trap with no cheese, I would say.'

'Yes,' he agreed sadly.

'I used to set a lot of traps as a boy. I remember one trap that we caught live field-mice with. We were young and rather bad and we used to bring the field-mice in our pockets to the dances and let

61

them out. They'd run into the middle of the floor and all the girls would jump onto the chairs. There'd be screaming and we'd be chased away and if we were unlucky sometimes we got. . . .'

Mr Schmidt arched his eyebrows and, pointing towards his rump, indicated a thrashing.

'Mr Schmidt?'

It was grandfather at the door.

'Herman Schmidt,' said the German, straightening his body and nodding his head. 'You are Mr O. Berne?'

'Yes I am. How do you do?'

After they had shaken hands, grandfather noticed the trap.

'What's that mess doing there?' he asked.

'Your grandson is going to grow up to be a famous hunter – aren't you Paul?' said Mr Schmidt, dropping his great hand onto Paul's shoulder and squeezing tightly.

'Take it outside. Get rid of it,' ordered grandfather.

Mr Schmidt lifted his hand from Paul's shoulder and followed after grandfather

'By the way,' he called from the hall, 'I recommend the use of chocolate as a bait. . . .'

The door of the front room banged shut and the low sounds of the men talking began to drift out. Paul glanced down at the mouse. Its smell was metallic and not unlike ragwort. He began to feel nauseous. The one thing he must not do, he realised, was to look directly at it.

He ran into the kitchen and found granny laying the tea-tray. The room was filled with the sound of cutlery clattering on porcelain.

'There's a dead mouse.

'Where?'

'In the parlour.'

'Don't be daft.'

The sugar hissed as she poured it into a china bowl.

'There's a trap.'

'There isn't any trap.'

'Grandfather said to take it outside and bury it.'

'What's the matter then? I'm too busy to do anything now. You do it! Take that.'

She waved towards the pail they used for the ashes. It was metal with staples the size of sixpences running down the side. The handle squeaked when he picked it up.

'Take the sweep too.' She indicated the grubby turkey's wing they used for sweeping down the top of the Aga. He picked it up

62

carefully, avoiding the clump of dried blood and cartilage where it had been snapped off.

'Off you go then!'

He returned to the parlour and set down the pail. The death smell was stronger than when he had left. He could taste it at the back of his throat. He dropped the turkey's wing onto the carpet and manoeuvred the trap onto it with his feet. A second later the trap slipped off the feathers and fell into the bucket with a dull clang. A cloud of ash rose, coarse and grainy. He peered inside and saw that the trap had landed upside-down. From under the pale wooden base with 'Made in Hong Kong' branded on it, snaked the grey, segmented tail. He jogged the bucket as if he were jiggling dice in a tumbler, turned the trap over and noticed with relief that ash had adhered to the ooze around the wounds.

Leaving the turkey's wing on a chair he went out to the vestibule. To the side of the umbrella rack where he stored his Dandy, Beano and Tiger Annuals, there was an odd wellington boot. He felt inside and pulled out a cob-webbed trowel. Granny used it for planting the spring bulbs. It had been kept there for as long as he could remember. Tugging on the front door he wondered where he would bury the mouse? The kitchen garden? The fields? The door swung back and a breeze glided in, flapping the coats hanging behind him. He went out onto the steps and stopped to ponder.

In the front garden there were two small lawns of coarse grass with stone pineapples on podiums. These had once stood on the gable ends of the big house grandfather had burnt down. Narrow flower beds lay beyond them where thorny rose bushes grew in the shadow of the coarse green hedge. The wind came again, stirring the longish grass like water and swaying the rhododendron bush in the field below. Suddenly he knew where he was going to do it.

He carried the pail out to the avenue and climbed into Black's field beyond. Black had been the name of the English settlers who had originally owned the estate. The first Black had been a Cromwellian soldier and the last had been Miss Black. It had been from her that his grandfather's uncle – a rich priest who had made a fortune in Australia – had bought the place. She had conducted business from her bed wearing a white parlour maid's hat on her balding head.

Descending the gentle slope at the field's edge, he recalled the last occasion on which grandfather had told the story. The transition from a Cromwellian soldier to an old lady bargaining with a priest, he remembered, had provoked sage mumblings and serious noddings of the head amongst the listeners. He had not understood why at the time and it still puzzled him.

He reached the side of the rhododendron bush and began to force his way in. The thick, dark green leaves reminded him dimly of rubber door wedges and the branches from which they grew seemed to share this mysterious rubbery quality. He penetrated the first screen of foliage and found himself in what he liked to think of as the outer chamber of the bush. He turned round and looked back over his shoulder. It was always his habit to check if anyone was watching when he went in. In the distance, the copper beeches were swaying, their grape-coloured leaves sparkling in the light. Below them stood the Red House. The lower half was faced with stone and here and there green fuzzy growths had spread across it, reminiscent of the slime on rocks at low tide. The upper half in contrast was plastered and painted cream and shone in the sun. The guttering was bright red. Closer to him stood the palings which he had just negotiated, a fence of wire stretched tightly between concrete posts. The section closest to the house was draped with the day's laundry; three sheets patched with big squares and a thick blanket. After washing them that morning, granny had forced them through her cracked yellow mangle, carried them out in a square wicker basket and hung them up. After that he knew she had come out once an hour to shift them because she feared the metal wires might leave a thin line of brown rust. At night, when the wind blew fiercely, the palings made whining noises that rose and fell like a wail of pain.

He stepped delicately through a pattern of interlacing branches, passed through another screen of leaves and at last found himself in the green, quiet place at the centre. Of all the hideaways that he used, this was the most important. In the days when he had first come to the Red House, when his yearnings for his mother had been at their most acute, it had not been in his bed, dozing in the early morning, or sitting under the umbrella rack in the vestibule reading his comic annuals, or even in the hollow in the hedge behind the pumping hut that he had found comfort, but in the rhododendron bush. Seated in the middle of the green chamber, staring out at the low blue hills on the horizon, he had always been able to forget his unhappiness, for a short time at least, and peace had always settled on him like a new fall of snow.

He set the bucket down on the always damp earth and peered into the bottom. In the green light the mouse was no more than a shadow lying on a dim square of wood.

Suddenly without thinking, he kicked the bucket. The metal

64

handle gave a dull clang and the mouse-trap jumped like a stubborn lump of flour in a sieve. He kicked the bucket again, and stooped down to look more closely. It was curious to think the creature had once been alive and had run around until it had received a sharp blow on the back of the head. Life had ended but had anything been left after? His father had not believed in the soul but his mother had. It had been a subject of bitter dispute and there had been one argument he had never forgotten. He had been in the kitchen of the London house. It had been evening. It had been the evening of the day he had finished making a small boat in his carpentry class at school. He had filled up the deep butler sink with cold water and pulled a chair to the side. He had stood on the chair and floated the ship. He had been very proud of it. It had been grey, with pointing prow and a very graceful stern which he had spent a long time cutting out and sanding down. For masts he had two pegs and for ballast he had half a wall-bracket screwed between them. As the vessel twisted and turned on the water, he had heard the sound of angry voices behind the serving hatch which connected the kitchen to the dining room adjacent. His stomach had tightened and he had felt like peeing. But that had been out of the question. It would have necessitated him going upstairs, and if his father heard him moving he might shout at him. He had pressed his groin against the cold side of the sink and continued to play with his boat, moving it in rather aimless circles.

Suddenly his father had stuck his large head covered with black wavy hair through the serving hatch and shouted, 'What are you doing?'

'I'm playing.'

'What are you playing with?'

'A ship.'

'Is it a battleship?'

'I made it at school.'

'Show me.'

Paul held up the grey, crude, dripping shape by the masts.

'Your mother believes in the existence of the soul,' his father had said, 'but it's balderdash and rubbish,' and with that he had shut the serving hatch with a slam.

Paul had gone on playing, his hands getting colder and colder. From beyond the wall came the loud noises of angry argument but nothing that he had been able to make sense of. After a while red mottled marks had appeared on his fingers and he had got down from the sink and had gone and sat by the stove on the string-backed

65

chair which his father had repaired with twine salvaged from parcels. He had put his hands on the grey enamel sides of the stove and sat back to wait for the return of warmth and feeling to his fingers. Abruptly the kitchen door had opened.

'Go up to bed,' his father had said.

'My hands are cold.'

'Go up to bed, I said.'

'Can't I go in a minute?'

'I said go to bed now.'

As he went into the hall he had seen his mother standing in the doorway of the dining room. She had seemed to be trying to hide herself away from him. Her eyes had been rimmed red; clearly she had been crying; and yet at that moment her face had been glowing.

'Goodnight mother.'

'Go to bed,' she had said.

Later, lying in his bed, he had heard laughter coming from his parent's bedroom and the obscure noises that accompanied their mysterious togetherness. The next morning, when he had gone to wake his mother to make him his breakfast before he went to school, she told him to go away.

'I'm staying in bed. It's too cold to get up,' she had said and curled up against his father dozing quietly under the blankets.

On the way to school, he had beaten the trees and fences which he had passed with a stick and he had arrived in class with both palms bruised and hurting.

He tipped the bucket onto the earth and tapped it on top as if he were making sand-castles. When he took the bucket away, there was a perfect circle of grey ash like a sun on the black ground, with the mouse lying in the middle fast asleep in the trap. If the animal had had a soul, he asked himself, then where did it go? And if it went somewhere, then the soul had to be something. Perhaps it was still inside waiting to be let out like a gas? He picked up the towel and began to prod with it. There were no signs of anything escaping as far as he could see. He laid the shovel on the neck. A sharp press, he imagined, and the mouse would fall open like a vegetable. He pressed but nothing happened. He pressed harder and through the handle of the trowel he felt the distant movement of shifting bones. Quite as suddenly as it had come to him his curiosity left him and he felt slightly nauseous again.

He bent down and began to dig. The earth came away in slivers like very cold butter. He wondered if his foot-steps had packed it down so tightly? Once the top-soil was away, progress was quicker.

An inverted cone began to appear. The shape was irritating. He wanted a square in the ground like a proper grave. He attacked the sides but all he achieved was a bigger cone. When the hole was deep enough, he rolled in the mouse and the trap together and covered them with earth. At the finish there was a small mound of dark earth. Ton . . . ton . . . ton . . . he struck with the flat of his spade. The mound became a bump. It was done. He looked through the leaves at the hills in the distance. Instead of the blue that he had always seen on those sad evenings when he had stared out, he saw the lower slopes were green and divided into fields and the upper reaches brown and red with bracken.

'Dear God,' he murmured to himself, 'I am sorry for what I did to the mouse. . . .'

He waited for a while to see if there was anything else he wished to say but nothing occurred to him. He picked up his things and headed back.

Throwing the bucket and trowel over the palings and climbing between two wires, he wondered what he was going to do? Could he go back inside? No! It was definitely too soon to go in. He gazed at the sky and then down the avenue. Pock-marked and rutted, it curved away from him, the palings hung with washing on one side and the lawn of grass, gorse and ragwort on the other. Small at the bottom stood the gates and smaller still, Andy's little cottage just beyond them.

Quite suddenly a vehicle pulled up beyond the gates. It was too early for the Limerick bus. He dropped the bucket and began to trot forward, running on the ragwort side, kicking every dandelion which he passed and sending clouds of white seeds scattering in every direction.

He reached the bottom breathless. In the wall beside the gate there was a set of steps. He carefully climbed the slippery treads, negotiated the lip of the stone at the top and jumped down the four feet to the ground on the other side.

Standing up and brushing off the gravel from the palms of his hands, he saw that it was a coach that had drawn up in front of Andy's cottage and that behind the windows there were strange faces staring at him.

What he took to be an arm beckoned. He stepped forward. 'Slattery's for Coaches' glowed ghost-like through the grey-silver road-dust covering the body. Here and there someone had written 'Wash me please' and 'I need a clean' with a finger.

He reached the middle window and saw a huge moon-face staring

67

down at him with pale blue eyes like a baby's. Above the face stretched a forehead high like the coiffure of Marie-Antoinette in the picture in his *World History of Revolutions* book which showed her ascent to the guillotine, except that instead of piles of hair, he saw skin stretched tightly over bone. Thick veins like worm casts curled up from the temples and here and there the skin ridged and dimpled as if there were no bone underneath. The hair on top was short and the nose, tiny in relation to the gigantic head, was dripping with dull grey catarrh.

The moon-faced boy turned to the figure sitting beside him and tugged his arm. An old man dropped his hands from his face and looked down towards Paul. His cheeks were sunken and his chin swooped upwards as though searching for his lips. His eyes were set very close together. He looked quite mad.

'Pah!' the old man seemed to mutter. He turned away and began to rock backwards and forwards.

The moon-faced boy tugged once more at his neighbour's arm.

'Pah!' the old man seemed to mutter again and he pushed the boy violently away.

The boy wiped his nose. A silvery smear like the morning trail of a snail appeared on his blazer. He smiled. It was a sad, vacant smile.

Rat-tat-tat! At the next window a fat girl with a red ribbon tied in her hair was standing on one of the seats. He saw that she was banging the secret part of her pelvis, the unmentionable part in which all the secrets were locked away, against the glass. The girl began to raise her dress. Clack-clack-clack went her buttons. Her thighs were pale and fat and vibrated with the force of her movements. When she raised the dress high enough he saw that she was wearing dark-coloured knickers and that there were black hairs curling out from under them.

The dress was as high as her waist. She leant back from the glass and tucked it into her knickers, forming a bulge in front of her stomach. She smiled at him. He stared back. She stroked her swollen belly and her lips moved, forming strange shapes reminiscent of eating.

At that moment a nurse in a blue cape and a white starched hat shot into view. The nurse grabbed the girl by her hair and forced her down in her seat. Attempting to stand up again, the girl began to batter with her wrists. The nurse's hat dropped off and a length of her hair came unpinned. The nurse pushed the girl down and struck her on the face. The girl sank back in her seat and began to wail. Paul found her expression without the sound of crying strangely terrifying. The nurse heaved her forward in the seat like a sack and tipped her head back over her shoulder-blades at an alarming angle. Paul saw the girl's eyes were slanted and that her nose was very small and turned up slightly at the end. Blood was pouring out. It was dark and thick. It ran down the shallow channel underneath the nose, along the top of her lip and down onto her chin. The mouth was open but none went in.

The nurse looked up and saw that Paul was watching. She had not noticed him before. His face began to turn red and his ears to burn. He knew he should turn round and run but he was never able to move when he was caught. On his face an expression of apology began to form. He knew this was fatal; he knew this encouraged adults to be even angrier than if he did nothing. But apologise was what his face always did. It was inevitable, like being sick or when his bowel movements were liquid and he was unable to stop them coming out.

The nurse shouted through the glass and waved her arms violently. The message was unmistakeable. Keeping his gaze fixed firmly upon her, he sidled sideways until he was out of sight. Then he turned and ran around the side of the bus.

As he emerged on the other side, old Andy came out from his cottage in a dark suit, black like a beetle, carrying a paper bag under his arm. He took a few tiny steps down the path, moving like a mannequin, then stopped and looked around himself blinking in the sunlight. Close behind him a second nurse appeared and began to fumble at the door with a large, black key. Andy called instructions over his shoulder to her but these did not appear to help. When she eventually finished Andy pointed towards the window sill with his stick and she put the key under the geraniums which grew there in an enamel tray. Andy handed over the brown paper bag and the nurse took him by the elbow. They began to walk.

A quick glance to the side and Paul saw that the other nurse was nowhere to be seen.

'Hullo Andy,' he called but old Andy did not appear to hear.

He ran the few steps to the front gate. Down the path Andy crept towards him, tapping ahead with his cane. He was wearing a suit so worn with use that it shone and so big that the jacket hung loosely from his shoulders while the trouser ends bunched up over his boots. Paul could remember Andy as never wearing anything else.

At Andy's side, the nurse spoke quietly and constantly: 'Come on now Mr O'Connor. Not far now Mr O'Connor....'

69

From time to time she looked up and screwed up her eyes, judging the distance that was left to travel.

When they drew near, Paul pushed back the already wide-open gate so that two could get through.

'Hullo Andy,' he said.

Andy stopped and looked up.

'Hello my fine young man. How are you today?' Andy was wearing his false teeth for the occasion and a whispering sound streamed after his words through the gap at the front.

'Very well thank you.'

'You're in finer shape than I am. They're taking me to a hospital.'

'Now, now Mr O'Connor.' It was the nurse. 'There's nothing to worry about. We're just bringing you in for a simple check-up. Nothing more.'

Andy pulled his arm free from the grip of the nurse.

'Do you see that Paul?'

He held up his hand. The fingers were locked into a bent position. It was more like a claw than a hand.

'I can't move them properly. . . .'

Andy moved the fingers feebly.

'Arthritis! All my little joints are seizing up and my big ones will soon be seizing too. Do you know Paul, what's inside each of these joints? There's a crystal. A little tiny crystal. That's what it is . . . arthritis . . . a little tiny crystal in the joints. . . .'

Paul gazed at Andy's hand. The skin was dark brown and shiny, reminding him of bog colour. Black hairs grew everywhere, wiry as bracken. On one finger, the dark trace of nicotine stain spread towards the knuckle.

'Never lose your health. It's the most important thing you have. You're not worth a box of matches without it.'

Rooks cawed in the trees behind the demesne wall, their calls constant and monotonous. Far away a donkey brayed, the hee-haw like an asthmatic wrench.

'Come on Mr O'Connor,' continued the nurse, taking him by the elbow. 'Standing here all day isn't going to do us any good, now is it?'

'I've known this one here since he was a nipper. Since he was that high.' Andy gestured first at Paul and then towards the ground with his stick.

'Yes Mr O'Connor. You must be very happy to see him grown up to be as big and strong as he is. Now, shall we go?'

'I want to give him something.'

70

'Certainly Mr O'Connor. But we can't wait too long. Everyone's waiting on us in the bus and we still have more calls to make.'

'It won't take long.'

'That's all right then.'

Andy wriggled his arm and the nurse let go of his elbow.

'I'll tell you a story about this one! I wonder if he remembers it?'

'Tell me Mr O'Connor.'

Andy handed his stick to the nurse and lifted off the green felt hat that he wore on his head.

'Well this one came down one winter's morning with his grand-mother. . . .' Contorting his arm into a strange position, Andy drew the finger ends of his crooked hand across his head. His hair was like a silvery-grey bathing cap, for all the hairs seemed stuck together.

'Do you remember that?'

'Was I very small?' asked Paul.

'You were very small.'

Andy set his hat back on his head and pulled it over his eyes.

'Well they came in, himself and his grandmother and they sat at the fire. It was cold outside. There was a frost. . . .'

Andy held up one of his hands as if he were a boxer.

'The earth was like that fist. It was as hard as iron.'

With his crooked fingers, Andy undid the buttons of his jacket with surprising ease.

'Well I made a sup of porridge for the breakfast and I brought it outside in a pan and I stood it on the garden wall behind to cool.'

He pulled open his jacket and insinuated his fingers into the top pocket of his black waistcoat underneath. A dull-coloured silver chain looped across his middle.

'And when I came back into my own kitchen the grandmother says to this one, "Ask Old Andy what you just asked me." This one looks at me and we hear this noise in the next room. "Is that the little wife making the beds?" says this one. "Is that the little wife making the beds?"'

Andy began to chuckle to himself as he pulled something out of his pocket.

'And do you know what it was?'

'No,' said the nurse.

'Wasn't it this big rat that had come in the night before from the cold and hadn't I locked it in the room. It was too quick for me to kill it.'

Andy began to laugh with his mouth open.

'Is that the little wife making the beds. . . .'

71

Inside his chest, phlegm moved in sympathetic spasms with his laughter.

'Have you got something for your young friend then Mr O'Connor?' enquired the nurse.

'Here you are Paul. . .' "Is that the little lady making the beds. . . ."'

He held out a shining florin and began once more to laugh.

Paul took the coin.

'Thank you,' he said. 'Thank you very much.'

The nurse handed Andy back his stick.

'Come on Mr O'Connor.'

They began to move towards the coach.

'Very good Mr O'Connor, very good. . . .'

They reached the steps and the other nurse appeared. Paul turned round on the pretext of shutting the gate so that he did not have to look her in the eye. When he turned back the first nurse was too busy helping Andy up the steps to notice him.

Andy was settled in a seat at the front. The driver banged the door shut and started the engine. The coach shook.

'Goodbye Andy. Thank you for my money,' called Paul.

The gears engaged with a deep-sounding clunk and the coach began to creep forward.

'Goodbye,' Paul called again.

He waved but Andy neither saw him nor heard him. He was staring through the front window of the coach and it seemed to him that Andy had already forgotten what had happened.

The coach went past. He glimpsed the faces staring down at him and dimly wondered if the moon-faced boy or the girl with the red ribbon were among them, but all the faces were a blur. As the coach drew away he saw that some of the patients were waving through the back window. He waved back and the exchange went on for some time until the coach disappeared around the bend. The rooks were cawing in the trees and the diesel engine still rumbled in the distance. He tied his two shillings in his handkerchief, stored it safely in his pocket and set off in the direction of the bog.

The front room was on the eastern corner of the house. The tall windows loomed in front of him. Turning his head he glanced quickly into the darkened interior and saw at once that grandfather's bony frame was not in its habitual chair. It was safe. He stopped and put his face to the glass. Mr Schmidt was sitting on the green button sofa smoking his pipe. He raised his arm and gave a thumbs-up sign and Paul nodded in return. The shop-bread sandwiches on the tray beside him were like pieces of candlewax.

The German formed his lips into a circle and exhaled a large cloud of smoke. It was blue and it hung in the air like morning mist rising from the bog. Mr Schmidt gave a little smile and looked upwards. He was staring at the plates above the curtain pelmet, on each of which there was a face that stood out. Paul knew just what he was seeing. During the hours he had spent in the room on various social occasions, sitting in exactly the spot where Mr Schmidt was sitting, he had studied them closely: the Chinaman with a pony-tail; the Arab with flashing eyes and a curved dagger between his teeth; the black man with tattoos on his cheeks; and the bronze-coloured man with a gold earring. They came from a series called 'Faces of the World' which had been advertised on the back of a cereal packet and for which granny had spent some months collecting the required tokens.

Mr Schmidt re-crossed his legs. Another wreath of blue rose from his pipe and hung in the air.

Paul turned away and began to walk along the side of the house. The next room along was the breakfast room. Large venetian blinds hung behind the windows, grubby and buckled. He turned the corner and found himself behind the meal house and the kitchen. A large bush with coarse green leaves grew out of a hole in the middle of the concrete flag. The dogs often itched their backs on its lower branches, and tufts of their brown and white fur hung down from it. In the wall behind was the tiny window of the box room. Through the mud-spattered glass he saw a crucifix on the wall inside and the black shape of an iron bedstead like a crouching dog. For reasons he had never fathomed his grandfather slept in the box room whenever he had to get up especially early.

He swung the bucket forward and hit the oil drum that stood by the window under the broken gutter. Brown slivers and particles of rust fell silently to the ground.

He peered forward and saw his face dark in the water. The reflected sky was very bright behind him.

'Aie.'

'Ai-ee,' came back the echo faintly.

He gathered saliva on his tongue and spat down. Ripples spread across the placid water.

Why did his granny use this water, he wondered, when she rinsed

73

his hair after washing it? There were shiny spots of grease on the surface and a sediment of rust on the bottom.

From inside the kitchen raised voices fluttered out. Leaving the pail by the drum he cautiously circled the meal house. On the other side the back door was open, and by inclining his head he was able to see through the scullery into the kitchen beyond. Grandfather was sitting in front of the Aga, a towel hanging on the rail beside him. A starched collar attached by a single stud hovered on the back of his neck like a gigantic butterfly. His trousers were rolled up to his knees, revealing calves like thin white rods and his feet standing in a basin of steaming water.

'Strike while the iron is hot I say!' came grandfather's voice from within.

The knobbly stones of the meal house were cold and damp through his pullover.

' . . . Never look a gift horse in the mouth. . . .'

'But we don't know who he is,' returned granny's voice along with a rattling of crockery.

She was tucked around the corner by the kitchen table where Paul was not able to see her.

'We haven't seen his credentials. He could be a charlatan for all we know, who travels the length and breadth of Ireland cheating every gullible farmer that he meets out of his land.'

Paul did not understand what they were talking about but he recognised it was important. He cupped his hand to his ear.

'I know an honest man when I see one,' grandfather called over his shoulder. 'There isn't a crooked bone in our German friend.'

'How do you know? And seeing as he's so honest, why's there the rush then?'

'We're just going to look at the deeds. It's just a reconnaissance. Nothing more.

'If I know you you'll sell the land for next to nothing today and we'll be out on the roads tomorrow.'

'He's only interested in the water meadows. He doesn't want the whole place . . . '

'He said he was interested in them as a starting point,' interrupted granny.

'They're useless fields to me and I can get good money out of him.'

'I'll believe that when I see it.'

'Listen here, lady know-all! What have you ever done in this line but buy and sell a few eggs? I have a nose for these matters. I know a profitable business transaction when I see one.'

As grandfather began to turn Paul darted back as quick as a fish in water. It was dangerous to eavesdrop but it was impossible to leave now. He edged forward again. Grandfather was staring down at the basin in which his feet rested.

'You're traipsing off to the solicitor,' came granny's voice, 'at five o'clock on a Saturday afternoon, to sell land to a man you've never set eyes on before in your life. . . .'

'Hitler was an honest man,' he heard grandfather retorting. 'The Germans were an honest people. They were flattened in the war but they've built themselves up again by hard work. Mr Schmidt is no crook coming from that.'

'Pah!' exclaimed granny and appeared in the doorway heading in the direction of the kitchen cupboard.

'Come back here,' grandfather called back after her. 'There's fire in my veins.'

In his stomach Paul felt the mysterious sensation.

'I predict you'll be back on the drink before nightfall,' came granny's voice and the sound of the cupboard door clicking shut.

'Come here I said.'

Through the doorway Paul saw his granny step up to his grandfather and stand in front of him.

'Will you pass me the soap?' he asked.

'You can reach it yourself.'

'Did you hear what I said just now?'

'I heard what you said.'

'And what have you to say?'

'I haven't anything to say.'

'I'm a reformed man. I'll never drink again. On my oath.'

'You mean it now, but in half an hour you'll forget your words in the first bar you come to.'

Grandfather reached up and took hold of granny by the waist and tugged her towards him.

Perhaps, Paul wondered, the mystery was going to be finally explained? He took half a step forward.

'Let go of me,' his granny said quietly.

'You're my wife aren't you? And aren't I your husband?'

Granny was right in front of grandfather with her back to Paul. All that Paul could see of the old man were his white legs disappearing into the basin of steaming water.

'This is not the time or the place.'

Suddenly, there was something at the bottom of granny's skirt waving upwards.

75

'Go down,' she shrieked.

Paul saw that it was grandfather's hand.

'There's fire in my veins lovey-do. . . .'

The wind whispered through the leaves of the copper beeches behind him. What should he do? His heart was beating. He ran his thumb between his fingers and it was wet there. Alongside the fear there was a strange sense of excitement in his stomach.

'Don't do that,' shouted granny. She pressed her knees together and half-squatted.

'Let's do it now.'

'Mr Schmidt will hear us and Paul will be back any moment.'

'Bugger them both.'

Grandfather's arm disappeared under granny's skirt. Paul could see the backs of her knees, and her lower thighs.

'Don't! Don't!' she shouted. She sank back towards the floor pulling grandfather and his chair with her.

'You ignoramus,' he shouted.

He let go and he and his chair tipped back the way it had come. As she hit the floor her foot caught the side of the basin and water splashed onto the red tiles.

'You're not worth a box of matches.' He stared at the Aga and shook his head.

Granny rolled onto her knees cumbersomely.

'You're a disgrace,' she replied.

She rose to her feet and he could hear her knees creaking. She brushed the front of her skirt. He felt vaguely cheated.

Grandfather prised a bar of square soap from the saucer and dropped it into the water. It was all so quiet suddenly. He heard the chickens clucking around their hut down the lawn.

'Only an animal would do as you have done,' came granny's voice and she shuffled from view back towards the kitchen table.

Grandfather rubbed soap between his toes.

'What about my conjugal rights?'

'Conjugal rights!'

From out of sight, came the creak of wood. It was granny sitting on the chair at the end of the table.

The kitchen fell silent. Paul leaned back against the wall of the meal house. In the little garden which they kept at the back, there were stunted crab-apple trees with copper-blue branches, the same colour as the lightning conductor which ran down the side of the house. Beside the garden lay the path to the side gate, strewn with cinders. The wind blew and little flurries of dust formed; little

76

miniature tornadoes, he thought, as they disappeared into the hedge.

He slunk back round the meal house and scampered under the bush of coarse green leaves. From the dark boughs around him the dog's fur hung in cobwebs. He stared down the lawn. Great islands of bramble, jutted out of the thistles and ragwort and somewhere in the middle, leaning heavily to one side, stood the chicken run made of green corrugated iron. He imagined it was the prow of a ship skimming towards him and the chickens clucking around it became the white crests of crashing waves.

He pulled down from the bough above a brown and white clump of dog's hair and held it to his nose. It no longer smelt of Rover and Lassie but of damp. It was always disappointing to him the way their fur so quickly lost its characteristic smell.

At last he heard the glad sound of activity at the front. He scuttled out from under the bush and made his way to the east corner. Grandfather and Mr Schmidt were walking towards the blue Peugeot parked in the avenue beyond the gate. Grandfather was in his green suit, the one he had worn when he had taken Paul to the races, and his green pointed hat. He was like a moving green spear.

'I am so glad you have the time now to facilitate me ... ' Mr Schmidt's words drifted on the wind.

Grandfather's reply was inaudible. He waved his hand and puffed out a cloud of white cigarette smoke.

The men turned out the gate and Paul dropped to the ground to avoid being seen. The flag was damp and smelt of stone. The doors of Mr Schmidt's Peugeot opened and shut with dull thumps and a moment later the engine started up with a sound like air-gun pellets rattling in a tin. Mr Schmidt was pointing the wrong way and his car began to reverse down the drive with a low whining sound.

The noise of the engine grew fainter until eventually, only the moan of the wind was audible.

'One, two ... nine, ten,' he counted.

He got to his feet.

At the bottom of the drive the Peugeot was disappearing backwards through the piers of the gate.

He dashed round to the bucket, picked it up and ran up the back steps.

'Hello granny. I'm back,' he called from the scullery.

He stepped into the kitchen. Granny was sitting at the zinc topped table staring out the window.

'I buried the mouse.'

77

'Good boy.'

He put down the bucket on the tiles. Nearby was the basin full of soapy water and a wet towel hung over the back of the chair grandfather had been sitting in.

'Why do you rinse my hair in rain water?'

'What lovey?'

'Why do you use rain water when you're washing my hair?'

'Because its softer darling.'

She let drop the corner of the nylon curtain she was holding and turned towards him.

'Do you love your granny?'

'Yes I do.'

'Will you always?'

'Yes, for ever and ever.'

She folded her arms around him and laid her head on his chest. He lifted up his hands and looped them round her bony shoulders. At the bottom of her neck there was a bony lump.

After standing still for some moments, he noticed that through his shirt his shoulder felt wet from her tears.

Chapter Four

He stood and stared up at the barometer. It hung outside the breakfast room by a piece of copper wire which had stained the wall behind in the shape of a triangle. There were insects inside the glass, lying along the bottom; little dark shapes, round and tight. The needle pointed upwards towards 'Fair to Middling'.

Remembering how his grandfather did it, he reached up and gave the front a tap. The insects jumped and the needle floated up to 'Promising', then fell back to where it had started. Every day, it was his impression, no matter what the weather was like, it was always 'Fair to Middling'.

'Who's that? Is that you, Paul?' came a voice from behind the closed door of the breakfast room.

He stood absolutely still.

'Paul. Come in.'

He grasped the handle and opened the door. Grandfather was inside lying stretched on the green sofa by the fire-place. They had not had a fire there for months and it smelt strongly of old ashes and vaguely of bird droppings which he tasted at the back of the throat. Joseph had told him there were starlings nesting in the chimney stack.

'What were you doing?'

'Nothing. Just touching the barometer.'

He paused on the threshold. Grandfather had his feet up on the arm-rest. The price tags were still stuck to the soles of his brand new shoes.

'Come in Paul.'

Grandfather waved him forward with the page of a newspaper. He glimpsed the words 'Newmarket' and 'Leopardstown' in capitals.

'Shut the door! There's a draught!'

As he performed his task, he was careful to avoid the pages of newspaper underfoot. It was grandfather's habit when he was reading the papers to throw each page as he finished it on the floor.

'Pass the biro.'

Grandfather waved towards the big table covered with a white cloth. The pen lay on a table-mat with a picture of a Venetian gondolier on it.

'What were you doing outside just now?'

Paul handed him the biro. 'Quinn's Funeral Home' was written on the side.

'Playing.'

'What?'

'Nothing. I was just playing . . . '

The clock ticked on the mantelpiece. He looked up at the statue beside it, a striding figure in a red coat and a top hat, a monocle in his eye and a leer on his face. On the plinth supporting him were the words 'Johnnie Walker Whisky'.

Grandfather lit a cigarette and threw the match into the scallop-shell ashtray resting on his stomach. The brown parts on the shell and the stains on his fingers were almost the same colour.

'Do you love your grandfather?'

Paul curled his toes and clenched his back passage.

'Yes,' he said.

Grandfather exhaled a cloud of blue smoke and stared up at him with large dark eyes, his small head resting on a greasy red cushion. His hair was white and spiky. Oh please, thought Paul, don't let it be that he asks me to sit on his knee.

'Say you love your grandpa.'

'I love my grandfather.'

'You love your grandfather very much.'

'I love my grandfather very much.'

Smoke streamed from grandfather's nostrils. On the wall above there was a picture of a cat and a puppy frolicking in front of an old wind-up clock. 'Playtime' read the inscription at the bottom.

'Your grandpa loves you very much. He loves you the most. Do you love him the most?'

'Yes,' said Paul and felt his back passage opening.

'You love your grandfather the most?'

The air slipped out of him noiselessly. 'Yes.'

'Good boy.'

Discreetly he sniffed the air, fearful of discovery, whilst his grandfather put his hand in the pocket of his smart new waistcoat and pulled out a crumpled note.

'Here, this is for you.'

Paul saw at once that it was a one pound note.

'Thank you very much grandfather.'

He took the money, a grubby, worn oblong with a grimy feel. It

80

would be impolite, he felt, to put it straight into his pocket so he let his arm fall to his side. What was he to say? He felt bored and his mind was blank.

'We're flush with cash now. Do you understand?'

He nodded sagely. He did understand. It was all to do with the German.

'That's only the beginning. . . .'

Grandfather waved towards the one pound note.

' . . . And you're going to have your slice of the cake as well. You can be certain of that . . . '

Paul nodded vigorously and smiled.

'When your grandpa's old, will you come back and look after him?'

'Yes.'

'Do you promise that?'

'Yes.'

'Will you come back even when he's sick and dying?'

'Yes.'

'You'll come back from England?'

'Yes.'

Grandfather refolded the racing page and took the biro from behind his ear.

'Thank you very much for the money grandfather.'

'That's only the beginning. And don't forget what you promised just now. Isn't a promise a promise?'

'Yes.'

Using his palm as a rest, grandfather began to mark the news-print with big wavy blue crosses.

'Thank you very much again.'

Grandfather nodded.

He turned about. A picture of his uncle in a scholar's gown and hat hung by the door. 'Gerrard Finnerty O'Berne, MA', it read at the bottom.

He picked his way over the scattered pages of newsprint and went out.

He went down the three steps as the door swung shut behind him, tinkling the bell overhead.

'Hello Paul.' Mrs Noonan greeted him from under the green and white post office sign.

'Hello Mrs Noonan.'

The woman in front of the counter turned and stared at him. He did not remember having met her before.

'Hailstones in Kerry, in July!' said the stranger.

'All is not well.' Mrs Noonan folded her arms and shook her head.

He put his hand deep into his pocket and pulled out a small moist square of green.

'Frankly, I put it down to the rockets and all the other things they've been shooting up . . . ' continued Mrs Noonan.

On the shelves there were birdcages and tins of syrup with lions on the front. Wellington boots and yard brushes with stiff quills like a hedgehog's back hung down from the ceiling. The shop smelt of new sacks and creosote.

'You can't send those things up and expect nothing to happen!'

He opened the green note and stepped forward.

' . . . And what can I do for you?' asked Mrs Noonan.

He slipped it under the grill.

'You're a rich man today! Where did you get that?'

'My grandfather.'

'Your grandfather!'

He looked at Mrs Noonan through the bars. Her face was broad and white, her black hair tied behind in a pony tail and on her upper lip was a faint moustache like perspiration.

'Aren't you a lucky boy?'

'Yes,' he agreed.

'He seems to be very shy,' said the stranger.

'You're not shy? Are you?' interrogated the Post Mistress.

He shook his head.

'What do you want to buy?'

'Can I change it please? Can I have it all in pennies?'

'I don't know if you can have it all in pennies. . . .' Mrs Noonan pulled out a drawer. ' . . . But I'll see what I can do.

She dipped her fingers into the wooden hollow in the till drawer and pulled out a pile of change.

'You might be in luck.'

Scus, scus came the sound as she began to count the coins out on the counter.

'Where do you go to school?' asked the stranger.

He looked up at her quickly. She was a short woman with crinkly yellow hair and two very big front teeth resting on her lower lip.

'I don't go to school.'

'But everyone goes to school.'

'I went to school in England.'

'What about in Ireland?'

'I haven't been to school in Ireland, but I will be going to school in the autumn.'

'Do you like school? Are you good at your studies?'

He shrugged his shoulders.

'Let's hope you like it.'

He turned round and saw a row of brown columns on the counter.

'Thank you very much Mrs Noonan.'

Long black hairs grew from a brown spot on her face and moved like wires.

'How are you going to carry them?'

'In my pocket.'

'I don't think that would be a very good idea. They're very heavy.'

She pulled an empty jam jar from under the counter.

'I think this would be better.'

He nodded assent.

'Will you help me then?'

He picked up a pile of coppers and began to drop them in. The first ones bounced on the glass and made a loud noise. But when a layer of coins were formed, their successors fell more softly.

'What's your name?'

'Paul,' he told the stranger.

'Here you are Paul.'

She clicked open her worn purse, burrowed around with nimble fingers and pulled out a fraying bus ticket, a safety pin and at last a penny.

'This is for your collection.'

He dropped the new copper into his jar and Mrs Noonan pressed down the self-sealing top.

'You won't drop it on the way home?'

'I shan't.'

'Tell you grandmammy I was asking for her.'

'I will.'

He opened the door and went out. The bell sounded behind him once again. Beyond the goods crowded in the shop window, he saw the heads of Mrs Noonan and the stranger bobbing together. He turned for home.

'Robinson Crusoe walked along the sandy beach of his island paradise. Suddenly Robinson stopped dead in his tracks. . . .'

Paul turned to the next page and found an illustration of Robinson drawn in black lines on thick spongy paper. Robinson Crusoe was wearing baggy trousers made of animal skins, a waistcoat and a pointed hat like a tea-cosy. He carried muskets, powder horns and a sword, and above his head he held a parasol also made from rabbit pelts. He was staring at a footprint in the sand. The caption underneath read, 'A Stranger's Footprint!' After all the years of solitude, at last someone had come to Robinson's island.

'Paul . . . !'

He lifted his head from his book.

'Yes.'

'Your dinner's ready.'

He turned round and looked over the hedge. Granny was standing on the blue stone steps outside the back door. She was holding one hand over her forehead to shade her eyes.

'Your lunch is ready,' she called and disappeared through the dark doorway.

He sat back on the thin cushion from the kitchen which he had untied and carried out that morning. He felt warm and lazy and uninclined to go in. He picked up his book.

'The footprints,' he read, 'led away from Robinson Crusoe along the beach and disappeared into the distance. Robinson stared in the direction in which they led, searching for a clue as to whose footprint it might be, but there was nothing in sight except for the ocean breakers crashing on the shoreline.'

He pulled a dark green sprig from the hedge and closed the book on it. The sky above was a deep blue with big clouds everywhere, white and wispy, like insubstantial piles of cotton wool. He lifted his arms into the air and yawned until he felt the muscles of his abdomen stretching tight. What a pity, he felt, that their skies were not like they were on Robinson Crusoe's desert island, always pale blue, and with never so much as a wisp of cloud on the horizon.

He rolled onto the warm grass and stood up.

'Paul, this is the last time . . . ' his granny called.

'Coming.'

The place where he had been reading was the corner where the green, corrugated-iron pumping hut stood. It was surrounded on all sides by hedge, and the hedge had been trained to grow in an arch over the step that led in and out. He liked the spot for its cut-off feeling.

He twirled one of the clothes-pegs on the line that stretched across and surveyed his possessions scattered on the grass: a thick copy of Robinson Crusoe with a red spine and a picture of Robinson on the front looking to sea through a telescope; one of the cushions from the kitchen chairs with ties at each corner; a half-drunk bottle of cream soda lemonade standing in the shade under the hedge; his jam jar full of brown coppers; and an upturned glass with a wasp buzzing dozily inside.

Granny would complain if he left the cushion on the grass. He picked it up along with the jam jar and the book and put them on the top of the hedge. It was such a still day there was no danger anything would blow away.

He bent down by the glass and reached one of his sandals from the path. When the wasp settled on the grass he whipped away the glass and hit it with his sandal.

Peering down, he saw the insect crawling lop-sidedly with stuff thick and wet oozing out of the striped side of the body. At the back the large, black, pointed probe was still noticeably intact.

Holding the glass by the rim he ground it down. The execution was noiseless. Through the bottom of the glass he saw the wasp flatten out and expand. When he lifted the glass away, the insect seemed to shrink back to its normal shape.

He worked the insect into the glass and carried it to the hedge separating himself and the lawn beyond. He tipped the glass and the wasp wafted into the long nettles which grew on the far side. In life wasps were so heavy as they moved through the air but in death they seemed as light as dandelion seeds.

He returned to where he had killed the wasp and beat down the earth and grass. Now it was certain that no remnant of the sting could remain and he was safe to walk his private island again in his bare feet.

He dipped underneath the overgrown arch of hedge and began to walk towards the house. The concrete flag was warm and powdery underfoot. He lifted his arm and touched the crinkled skin of his armpit. Wet came away on his fingers and it smelt to him of vegetable soup. How strange an odour. His mother's smell had been milk mixed with beige-coloured face make-up and perfume. His father's was oily, like lanolin. So was granny's. As he walked, he could feel a cold trickle of sweat running over his ribs.

Rover rose from his spot, yawned and ambled towards him. His red tongue drooped out of the side of his mouth.

'Good dog. Good dog Rover.' He patted him on the head and the dog moved his tail.

He began to mount the steps, blue-stone and very cold. They were like icy water in the morning. He imagined they were taking all the heat out of his body, sucking it through his soles like a magnet. He thought of his mother and the earth around her. Was it cold in the coffin? he wondered and disappeared inside.

As he came into the scullery after finishing his lunch he knew there was something wrong. He felt it between his shoulder blades. He ran to the open door and looked across the flag. His heart began to thump. It was gone! He jumped down and began to run. Perhaps he had been mistaken? At a distance it would be hard to make it out. After all, one did see through glass!

He stopped about ten feet in front of the hedge. Robinson Crusoe was there, the dark green sprig that was his marker poking out from between the pages; and the cushion from the kitchen was there. But the jam jar was gone.

There was one last hope. He ran around to the other side in case it had fallen where he had been reading. But there was nothing, only the impression left in the grass where he had been sitting and the bottle of cream soda lemonade tucked out of sight.

The pipe that stuck up by the side of the cattle trough on the lawn nearby began to shake. The pipe was metal and so was the trough and the two banged together with a clattering sound.

He ran back to the flag, dropped onto his knees and peered inside the hedge. All that he could see was a tangle of branch and stick. He put his hand through and began to burrow around the bottom. He felt thin leaves, powdery earth and brittle twigs but not the cold solid feel of the jam jar. He was in pain. At the same time he wanted to scream and to cry; to hurt himself against the corner of the hut; and to throw his Robinson Crusoe at the dogs.

A wheezing noise came out of the end of the pipe. An animal lowed in the distance. Water began to spurt and splutter into the trough.

He sank back onto his haunches and pulled out his hand. There were scratches all over the back and from the deeper grazes blood was oozing. He wet the ends of his fingers and wiped saliva on his cuts. He put his finger back in his mouth for more moisture and tasted the metal taste of blood. The pain was growing stronger. He lay back on the warm flag and curled his knees up to his chest. Would the dogs come over and comfort him? He wanted to put his arms round their necks and bury his face in their long fur. They were lying outstretched, brown and white shapes to him. Quite suddenly the tears began to flow. They flooded out of his eyes and ran warm and hot down his cheeks. After the first tears which came easily, he felt a wringing sensation in his stomach. The pain of the contractions ran through his body in ripples. More tears came, trickling now. His nose felt blocked. He opened his mouth to breathe and tasted the familiar salty taste on his lips.

The hurt began to go. It was wet on the flag underneath his cheeks and he moved his head. there were tears between his eyes stopping him from closing them; a watery barrier. Through the slit he saw the flag as a dull fuzz and the unfaithful dogs as blobs. He wiped away the eye-wet on his sleeves and curled up tighter. To lie still now was the only recourse. The contractions still rippled but with less frequency. In the intervals there was just the ache. At the edge of his mind it occurred to him that he had been stupid and foolish to have left the jam jar full of money out at lunchtime, but he pushed the idea aside. If he dwelt on it the tears would only come back. He had to sink into a sort of numb grey state somewhere between sleep and wakefulness.

Behind him the cattle were at their trough. He could hear the hooves clopping on the stones around it, their heavy, thick furry necks rubbing on the metal rim, the slurping sound of their drinking. . . .

The grey sense began to settle. . . .

'Paul! What are you doing lying on the ground?'

He opened his eyes and saw his granny standing above him. She was carrying a meal bucket and Rover was trying to poke his nose into it.

'Go down,' she said swinging the bucket at the dog as a warning. 'Do you feel sick?'

He opened his mouth to speak and immediately began to cry again. The tears came out hot and big and he put his knuckles in his eyes to stop them.

'Go down you bold dog,' he heard his granny saying. A moment later there was a yelp of pain.

'I left my jam jar on the hedge,' he cried, 'and when I came back it was gone.'

'That was a stupid thing to do.'

'I had all my money in it. I had all my pennies.'

87

'Was that the money your grandfather gave you?'
'Yes.'
'You left it on the hedge?'
'Yes.'
'That was a very stupid thing to do.'

He heard her setting the bucket down on the flag and felt her taking him by the wrists.

'Stand up now. Come on.'

He let himself be pulled to his feet and opened his eyes.

Rover was at the bucket again with his nose right in it.

'Get down.'

She stamped her foot and Rover bolted away with his tail between his legs.

'That was a very stupid thing you did, leaving money on the hedge. You don't go leaving money lying around where tinkers or any passers-by can help themselves. You should know that by now!'

He felt the contractions in his stomach and began to wail: 'I want my money back....'

'Stop being such a cry-baby. I'm ashamed of you. Stop that at once or I'll send you to bed for the afternoon.'

She picked up the bucket and re-crossed the flag. Rover leapt up and down around her and she warned him off by swinging it at him. Lassie, in the shade on the far side, stood up and shook herself.

He wiped his eyes with his wrists and pressed them against his mouth.

Granny stepped over Rover's yellow bowl and bent down.

'Go down,' she called.

As the dog slunk off she tipped in a mixture of milk and solids.

She stepped away. Rover ran forward with his lips curled up at the edges so that his teeth showed and lunged into the bowl. He got something solid between his teeth, jerked his head back and swallowed it whole.

He closed his eyes and touched them with the ends of his fingers. The sus-sus of the water stopped. He opened his eyes and saw a bullock run his big hairy pink tongue around his lips.

Granny bent over the blue bowl beside which Lassie stood obediently waiting.

'Good dog,' she murmured.

With an alert expression, Lassie watched her meal splatter into her bowl. Granny stepped away. The dog moved forward, put her nose into the milk and delicately began to lap.

'I hope you've learnt your lesson,' granny called.

He nodded and made a noise which he hoped she would take as a 'Yes'.

She climbed the blue stone steps and disappeared into the kitchen. He ambled forward. Rover's bowl was almost empty. Just a small amount of milk and bits of speckled potato skin lay in the bottom. In Lassie's he saw green cabbage left over from their lunch, meal and bacon rind. The milk in which it all floated was a day old and smelt putrid.

Rover came from his empty bowl and put his head over the rim of Lassie's. Their tongues moving together were dark red and the flesh at the side like a cock's comb was a purple colour. It wobbled as they ate. Once, he remembered, he had tried to steal Rover's dinner so that he could give it to Lassie who had had none. Rover had bitten him on the palm and he still had a white scar from Rover's teeth on the fleshy part under the thumb.

He walked back to his private enclosure by the pumping hut and dropped his cushion on the ground. The dogs were yawning and their paws scratched on the flag as they settled down. He opened his book and leant back.

'Robinson Crusoe . . . ' he read, 'was walking along the beach . . . '

He looked from the book to the hut, the green paint peeling off the corrugating and then up to the sky, blue with huge piles of cloud sailing across it. He tried to see faces or objects in the white shapes above but he was not able to see anything, only the clouds as they were, moving like old-fashioned sailing ships across the blue, still sea.

Chapter Five

'Bring it up to the men,' his granny called.

The cardboard box stood on the kitchen table. He delved his fingers underneath and lifted it up. Inside there was a lemonade bottle full of milk with a red rubber stopper; enamel plates piled with slices of thick buttered bread, muslin cloths stretched over them; all the chipped and second-best cups that they had in the house; and an enamel tea-pot.

Granny emerged from the pantry wrenching the top off a bottle of Lea and Perrin's sauce.

'You'll be very careful?'

'Oh yes.'

He crossed the kitchen and tripped down the blue stone steps. Outside the flag was scorching. He went to the side gate and carefully passed the box through the rungs. The rusty spars were warm and bits flaked off as the box grazed against them. In the pale blue sky the sun stood high and there were few clouds to be seen. It was almost as good as a Robinson Crusoe sky. It had been hot for weeks and the night before he had slept with only a sheet and blanket.

He ran past the fallen tree which had been struck by lightning, its white bleached roots sprawling down like serpents and into the yard. All was still except for a gelding breathing noisily and making a clatter as he stuck his head over the half-door to see who was coming. A moment later he disappeared and his long tail swished in the darkness of the stable like the rustle of a dress.

He stepped forward, subdued by the quiet of the afternoon. The middle of the yard which was usually a morass of mud and filth had been baked hard by the heat and everywhere lengths of mud stood up like railway tracks. Around the edges the cobblestones were grey squares like the markings on a tortoise. A solitary brown hen moved across them, pecking in the crevices.

He went through the gate on the other side of the yard and he found himself in the Bog Road. Elm and ash towered on either side and it was cool there and the light was green. He looked up. The leaves were vivid from the sun and the tiny veins which ran across them showed up like fish-bones.

He heard sheep calling, a dull sound strangely irritating like the buzz of a bluebottle nudging against glass. The meadow beyond was filled with them, their fleeces not white but a grubby off-white, the colour of wet cotton sheets, and all with their heads down as they dragged their front teeth across the grass making a noise like a comb dragging through hair. By the gateway stood the sheep-pit, rank and poison-smelling.

The road ran straight through a succession of fields and then curved at right angles at the bottom of what they called Waterman's Meadow. A large oak stood about halfway up that sloping field and it was reputed it had been a gallow's tree in the penal times. It was huge with spreading branches that were thick like the timbers of a house.

Once he had sheltered under there in a storm and had felt frightened remembering what he had been told. He had imagined there were skeletons in the dark branches overhead waiting to jump down and strangle him. He had stared upwards but all he had been able to see had been a tangled mass of foliage and occasional forks of lightning. In the end he had given in to panic and squelched down the field in the pouring rain. Into the Bog Road he had turned and along he had gone under dripping trees. Darker and darker, wetter and wetter. It had been then he had heard the clatter of the skeleton's bony feet on the stones behind him. Over his shoulder he had stared back but there had been nothing behind him only the dark road and waving greenery. Half-looking forwards, half-looking backwards, stumbling because he was not looking either way properly, he had slithered and slipped his way towards safety. His face had got hot; the rain had run under his collar; and he had arrived at home cold and hot, shivering and feverish. Mercifully, in the sun early on a summer's afternoon, the gallows tree did not look like the tree he had been so frightened under. . . .

He rounded the corner and the Bog Road began to twist and turn whilst on either side the banks grew higher, so high that he was not able to see over them into the fields beyond. A donkey brayed in the distance and he began to hear the faraway shouts and calls of the men. The calls grew louder. He came round a bend and saw through an open gateway the Ten Acre Field stretching away from him, a gentle slope of yellow stubble. Grandfather and the harvesters were on the skyline, their thin bodies dark against the sun.

He went through the gate and began to climb the hill. Even through his sandals he could feel the sharp ends of the stubble. He began to feel hot and he sensed trickles of sweat running from under his arms down his ribs. His blue cotton shirt was sticking uncomfortably to his back. He put down the box and pulled the shirt away from the skin. Coolness and relief immediately followed. He stared up the shorn, yellow field. At the bottom it had looked as though the men had been dancing, but now he could see they were cutting the grass with scythes and forking it into ricks. A horse and cart stood by waiting to be loaded.

He carefully picked up the box and continued upwards. A cabbage white butterfly floated by, its movements seemingly erratic. He drew closer to the workmen; the air seemed to be getting dusty.

'Jesus!' shouted a man who began to run down the field towards him, brandishing a pitchfork. There was something dark scurrying along the ground in front of the man.

'Hah!' shouted the man and he threw the pitchfork. It bounced on the hard earth with a twang, somersaulted and fell flatly.

'What was it?' someone called.

'The biggest rat!' replied the man. 'Big as a cat.'

Paul stared in the direction of the pitchfork and shivered. He could see nothing moving, but in case the rat was making towards him he moved sideways and took the path by the edge.

'Have you brought the tea?' called across the man who had thrown the pitchfork as he bent to pick it up.

'I have.'

The others at the top turned towards him.

'Good lad,' came the voice he recognised as his grandfather's. 'Hurry up here now, we're thirsty.'

The men moved in a bunch towards the horse and cart and carefully laid their tools on top of it. The horse, a large grey gelding with big flanks, pawed the ground with his heavy legs. By the time he drew close they were talking in huddles and several were smoking, sending white, pungent-smelling clouds of Woodbine and Sweet Afton into the hot summer air.

He put the box down on the cart. The scythes and the pitchforks lay in a cruel tangle. Strong brown arms reached into the cardboard, some with dark blue anchors or dull red hearts tattooed on them and all sprinkled with a fine dust and with bits of straw caught in the hair. He felt someone touching the back of his head.

'You're very good to carry this lot up,' he heard his grandfather saying.

'Good man indeed,' said another voice.

Joseph, on the other side of the cart, was smirking and nodding towards him. His gold-rimmed glasses were misted up, and there were particles of dust stuck to the insides.

He noticed there was a strong smell of sweat. It was a sour smell reminding him of rotting apples in the autumn. The muslin cloth was taken off the plates and big hands on thick wrists began to reach for slices of bread. The butter was warm and soft and more than usually yellow. A wasp floated in.

'Kill it,' ordered a voice.

Someone swished the cloth in its direction. The wasp swerved away.

'You'll just make it angry that way, you eejit!'

The cups were lined up in a row. The enamel tea pot was held above them and the dark tea was poured out without a stop between each cup. Dark steaming puddles formed on the wood of the cart.

'You're wasting it.'

'Oh there's plenty. Don't be such an old woman.'

The stopper came off the milk. Wet teaspoons began to dig into the white sugar, staining it brown like iodine sprinkled on snow.

'Would you do me a favour, lad?'

He looked up. It was a big man with freckles who had asked the question.

He nodded.

'Would you bring that fella a cup of tea?'

On the far side of the cart a man stood with his back to everyone smoking a cigarette.

'I will,' he said.

'How many sugars?' called over the man with freckles.

'Two. Heaped,' replied the fellow with his back turned.

The freckled one hitched up his trousers and stirred the tea.

'Slice of bread?' he called.

'Okey dokey,' replied the other.

There was a little talk. Everyone was blowing on their tea and taking short, hot gulps.

He took a cup and two slices from the freckled man.

'Good lad you are.'

He began to walk round the side of the cart. As he passed him by Joseph dipped his bread into his tea and began to suck it noisily.

'You animal,' said someone.

'If you want to know how many toes a pig has, take off your own boots and count,' replied Joseph.

There was a murmur of laughter.

93

'Speak for yourself, Joseph.'

The man with his back turned was in front of him like a captain on board ship staring out to sea. He was wearing a white shirt with wet stains around the arms and a pair of coloured braces.

Paul cleared his throat. His feet were itching. Little points of straw had stuck through his socks and were pricking the skin underneath.

'Excuse me sir,' he said, 'I have some tea for you.'

The man let out a bellow, raised his arms into the air and swung around as if he were a demon bearing down on him. The man's face, from his hairline to his chin was completely purple, the same colour as a blackberry stain; his nose was enormous and shapeless like a cauliflower; and his blue eyes staring out from between purple lids were the only recognisable human feature. Paul shrieked and the tea flew from his hand.

The man with the purple face began to leer towards him. The sound of mirth appeared to be coming out of his mouth. Around the cart behind him Paul was dimly aware of further laughter, big pent-up laughs. He moved to the side and began to run. Someone called, he thought, but he paid no attention. The earth was hard underfoot and he could feel the stubble.

'Paul . . . Paul . . . come back. We didn't mean it!'

He looked back and saw grandfather was running after him, desperately waving his arms. There were others with him; heavier, bulkier, younger men. One of them was the man with the purple face.

'Come back Paul, come back,' his grandfather called. 'The Strawberry didn't mean it. He wants to apologise.'

The men around the cart were shouting too and gesturing desperately.

He looked forward again. The gate lay open, the Bog Road stretching beyond, cobbles gleaming like silver in the darkness under the trees. He would not stop. They would not catch him. He would run on and on. He would run for ever. Through the gate he would go and along the Bog Road; along the Bog Road into the yard; through the yard and then down to home; to the Aga murmuring; to the pantry smelling of marmalade; to the kitchen table which would be dusted with flour from the scones which his granny made every afternoon.

Down the field behind someone was pounding. Faster! he urged himself. There was a stitch in his right side, a feeling as though all the muscles had torn apart and he was getting breathless.

'Stop will you!' someone shouted.

He felt a hand squeezing his shoulder. It was useless to go on. He stopped abruptly and the freckled man carried past him.

'It was only a joke.'

His face screwed up and tears welled up in his eyes.

'Oh don't do that!'

The tears began to trickle down his cheeks. He blushed and pressed his wrists against his eyes.

'It was meant to be a laugh! We didn't mean you to be frightened. Honestly. . . .'

He swallowed and nodded. He knew they liked it when he nodded.

'My little fellow. We didn't mean to give you such a turn.' Grandfather was behind. He felt the old man's thin, scraggy arm resting on his shoulder.

'Come on now. Come back up. It was just some innocent fun.' Grandfather spoke in a bark and in his eyes he looked angry.

'Yes! Innocent fun. That's right,' agreed the freckled man. 'Just innocent fun, wasn't it lads? he called.

'Yes,' chorused several voices.

He felt his grandfather turning him round and pointing him up the hill. His feet moved obediently. The hands were standing around the cart. The Strawberry stood on one side. He was turning something on the ground with his foot. Paul felt everyone was staring at him. He looked down as if he were looking where he was going. The earth was brown and cracked in places.

'It was only a joke. . . . We didn't mean any harm. . . . It wasn't as bad as all that. . . .'

He felt big hands slapping him on the back and ruffling the hair on his head.

'I'm so sorry for what happened,' muttered the Strawberry, towering over him. Between dark purple eyelids, Paul saw the pair of normal blue eyes again.

'No hard feelings.'

The Strawberry was holding out his hand. Paul put his own hand against the hot, calloused palm.

'Good lad you are,' called everyone. 'Good lad you are for not harbouring any grudges.'

'Oh yes, he's a good lad,' echoed grandfather. 'And because he's such a good lad and because he never carries tales, he's going to have a treat. Would you like to travel back on the hay-cart with Joseph?'

He nodded.

'Then you will, seeing as you're such a good lad and won't be carrying any tales to your grandmother. You won't, will you now?'

'No.'

The men emptied their dregs. Little wet marks spattered the earth, making it darker.

'Back to work gentlemen.'

The tools were taken up. He heard wood knocking against wood and heavy sighs.

'My back is killing me,' someone said.

'Rest up tonight and don't go on the bones.'

'How would I manage that with my wife fifty miles away . . . ?'

The hands sloped away towards the uncut grass. It grew across the field like a green curtain, as sheer as a cliff. A rabbit ran out, a small dark grey-coloured creature, and moved through the stubble.

'Whey,' went the shouts.

A couple of forks were waved. The rabbit skeetered sideways and disappeared down a gully with ungainly movements, its white fluffy tail waving behind.

'Should have had a gun, Mr O'Berne. Could have got that for the pot.' It was Joseph grinning behind his perpetually misted spectacles.

'Come on. Let's get this rick aboard.'

Joseph and another hand piled everything noisily into the cardboard box.

'Careful now. Go easy,' advised grandfather.

'Yes Mr O'Berne.'

Joseph turned and dropped the box noisily on the earth.

'You eejit.'

'Nothing broken Mr O'Berne.'

'I'll break you one of these days. I hope you can drive a cart better.'

Joseph scurried under the front and fiddled with something.

'Heave ho! Up she goes.' The floor of the cart tipped up and slid back on rails.

His grandfather drew cord from a dispenser. When there was sufficient he looped it over the rick standing just behind the cart.

'Right you are,' he called.

Joseph and the other hand turned the capstans and the rick began to move, jerking slowly up the incline like a turtle struggling out of the sea. Paul was reminded of an evening in England long before when he had watched the red roof of a boiler as big as a house bobbing above a row of trees as a huge lorry carried it along on its trailer.

The floor of the cart began to move like a scales about to tip. Joseph and the hand moved forward and took hold of it. The floor of the cart swung down and hit the chassis with a dull thump. The horse shied and the rick shivered, scattering yellow wisps. The job was done. The flaps at the side were raised with a clatter and the pegs dropped into place.

'All set to go.' His grandfather came behind him. 'And don't go carrying any tales, do you understand?'

His grandfather took him under the arms in the ticklish place. He braced himself for embarrassed laughter but none came. He floated upwards until his feet found the wooden edges. His grandfather pushed him forward. He fell chest first on the side of the rick, sharp ends pricking him through his shirt, the musty smell and taste of the hay in his mouth.

'Get yourself onto the top.'

He wriggled into place and looked around. The field was like a shorn head. He could see the contour of the land underneath. The gelding was fat and almost as wide as the stays that held him.

'And here, take this with you!'

He took the box from his grandfather and put it down in the straw. From the top of the field came the whistle of scythes cutting through grass and the clatter of the rakes bumping on hard earth. The cart moved up and down as Joseph climbed aboard.

'All hitched up properly?'

'Oh yes Mr O'Berne. Everything's ship-shape.'

Joseph took off his glasses and wiped the lenses.

'Bye Paul.'

'Goodbye grandfather.'

Joseph released the brake and shook the reins.

'Gee up.'

The horse moved slowly forward and Paul felt the familiar sensation of a cart on the move. His grandfather turned and began to walk up the field, carrying his scythe over his shoulder at a jaunty angle. Tall and thin, he moved nimbly, the huge dark shadow of his elongated body and the scythe over his shoulder, sweeping up the yellow field behind him.

Joseph drove the horse across the slope. When they reached the bottom he performed a U-turn and they approached the gate by skirting the lower fence. Paul took a piece of hay and began to pick his teeth. Everyone always seemed to do this when they were near

97

hay. As a practice it puzzled him; he did not find it pleasant. In the hedgerow there were brambles. The fruit was red and hard and, he knew, sour-tasting. But in a few months it would soften and turn black and what times he would then have, collecting it in a saucepan with his grandmother, tasting the sweet black fruit, staining his fingers and his lips with its colour.

The horse slowed and turned through the gate. In the Bog Road it was colder and stiller. The metal-shod hooves rang loudly on the stones below. In a beam of sunlight he could see a swarm of midges hovering. There was a damp smell. He undid the stopper on the lemonade bottle and put the end to his lips. The milk was warm and slightly sour. It left a funny taste on his teeth. He held the bottle over the side and emptied out the remaining drips.

'Are you all right up there?'

'I am,' he called back to Joseph.

He pushed the box down into the hay to minimise the danger of it falling off and lay down on his back. The straw was prickly and he moved from side to side until there was a space in which he was able to lie comfortably. Trees arched overhead and through the gap between the leaves and the branches, he saw the blue sky stretching away for ever. Below him the cart swayed, creaking gently like a boat, and he heard the reassuring sound of Joseph muttering, 'Up you go my girl', the leather reins clacking against each other, the rumble of the wheels. How peaceful it was. Nothing could be better than lying on hay still warm from the sun, the sky shining far above, cool dark trees on either side and a cart moving below.

He held a long wisp of hay in front of his face and began to open and shut one eye and then the other. The effect was to make the wisp jump from side to side. Joseph began to sing:

'Will ye go, Lassie, go. . . .'

Paul closed his eyes and let himself be rocked back and forth.

'All around the blooming heather. . . .'

Joseph stopped singing and began to whistle plaintively and slightly out of tune. There was distant bird-song in the trees. Sunlight filtered down, warm and healing on his eyelids.

Suddenly he felt a surge and noticed an unpleasant change in the character of the sounds below. He opened his eyes. The greenery was racing overhead, green and blue joining in a blur and in the box the crockery was clattering.

'Hold on now. Steady on girl. Come down here Paul. . . .'

Joseph's arm waved at the end of the rick, urging him forward. He was a swimmer perched on a rock in the middle of a stormy sea.

The box rose into the air beside him and all the crockery flew out in an arc. His hand was holding a piece of coarse twine and he felt it cutting into his palm. He had found it without knowing how. On the Bog Road behind him the cups shattered like snowballs and the plates rolled into the verges.

'Come down! Come down to the front. . . .'

Joseph's hair was sticking up and his face was red. Paul began to edge towards him. There was a surge and he was carried forward. It was like being moved by a wave up a beach. He was at the front. Joseph half-pulled, half-held his legs and he slithered down. His feet found the wooden seat.

'Sit down,' shouted Joseph pushing him on the shoulder. Joseph squatted down, hung his legs over the side and tucked them under the floor, so minimising the danger they would be caught. Brambles and bushes flew by, dangerously close. Joseph heaved on the reins. He leant against the rick and felt behind for a piece of twine onto which he could hold. Joseph was tugging at his knees.

'Sit down. . . .'

The cart lurched violently from one side to the other. Joseph leant back on the reins. The leathers were straight like rods. The cart lurched again. The horse lashed back with his legs, thumping the bottom of the cart.

'Sit blasted down. . . .'

He noticed he was moving sideways and downwards. He felt strangely weightless. Out of the corner of his eye he was aware of the sharp bend at the bottom of the Waterman's field looming ahead. Joseph was shouting incoherently. The horse wriggled frantically inside his collar like a fish on a hook. Paul's bottom was touching the wood. The next task was to swing his legs over the edge. The cart lurched sideways again. They were rattling towards the bend at top speed. Suddenly he slipped and before he knew what was happening he found himself caught between the back legs of the horse and the front edge of the cart. He felt the back legs of the horse pressing against him, felt the coarse fur rubbing his naked arm, felt the heavy thick rounded muscle pressing him and it was as if all these were events that were happening a long way away from him, like something witnessed through a telescope held the wrong way. He looked down and saw his feet dangling below and the hooves of the horse at the end of thick legs, sparking on the stones of the Bog Road. He felt Joseph grasping his neck at the junction of the shoulder. He was aware of fingernails digging into his skin and the skin seeming to stretch. Above his head there were shouts,

99

incoherent and desperate, whilst the wheels and the axle groaned below. A dreadful sound. The wheels of hell. Impossible to think with the heavy back legs of the horse pressing harder, squeezing his insides. He felt the wooden edge of the cart creeping up his body. It was like a rising line of water as one steps out deeper into the sea. The hooves were getting closer and the stones of the Bog Road were catching his heels. He lost a sandal. Behind the axle was turning. The wheel, the axle, the spokes of the wheel. Catch his legs in those and they would snap like a chicken's drumsticks. No. No. Not that. He must not fall. He struggled to lift himself onto his elbows. The cart cracked again. Sound of wrenching, wood and iron. Out of the corner of his eye he saw the bend in front and they were hurtling into it. The bony parts where the horse's back legs bent in the middle were pressing into his arms and his shoulders. Terrible wrench, a shower of splinters like a flurry in a snow-storm, a winding bang as he hit the ground, his bare legs dragging over sharp rocks, skin grazing away like chips of wood gouged with a chisel, something on his head, the hoof pressing, looking up, the gelding's intimate underbelly with private parts of grey skin the colour of an elephant, noise overhead rolling away, smell of grass, sweet and moist, sound of something bumping down the road, the gate, Waterman's field, the Gallows Oak, length of wood lying in front of him with a torn piece of leather attached to it, smell of grass, mould, twig, four iron hooves galloping by, something clattering after, boots coming towards him, one of the shoelaces undone, Joseph's face with his spectacles askew, 'Are you all right Paul?', a long silence, footfalls approaching, head being propped on something, grandfather's face and angry eyes, ' . . . Catch him! Catch that horse!', feet and hooves running together, blue sky above the trees, trees growing fuzzy, sky sliding, sliding away, 'Look at this collar! It's repaired with wire', dropping soundlessly into the sea, 'No! It was stung. It was a hornet', sinking slowly, water getting colder and darker, 'The wire stuck in the horse's side. No wonder he bloody bolted', reaching sea-bed, landing gently, sand clouding water, 'It was stung. It wasn't the wire', 'Bollocks!', someone crying and sniffling, Joseph standing away from the others, his mother treading towards him, flurries of sand around her feet, her knees, her face bending close to his, lids sinking, sinking, sinking, light closing out. . . .

Chapter Six

It was a hot afternoon. A bluebottle buzzed behind one of the yellowing venetian blinds. Perhaps I should get out of bed and kill it? he thought. His left shin was hot and prickly. He ran his other foot up and down, bumping over the big scabs that had formed all over it. At the same time he looked around for a suitable weapon. His annuals lay on the floor not too far away. They were a possibility, although a little unwieldy. He would have to wait until the fly was in the middle of one of the bedroom's small window-panes before he struck. What he really needed was a newspaper. There was one lying in the fire-place dusted with soot. He imagined how the soot would get on his hands and then from his hands onto the sheets. No! It was more trouble than it was worth. He lifted up the glass beside his bed and put it to his lips. The water tasted warm. Outside the sun was beating down. He lay back on his pillow and closed his eyes....

Hearing the door scraping back, he opened them again.

'Look who's come to see the patient,' said his granny.

He turned his head on the pillow and saw Philomena standing on the other side of the room. She was wearing a yellow dress with a white belt around the middle and from her shoulders hung a pale blue caridgan.

'Say "hullo" then to your cousin,' urged his grandmother.

'Hullo Philomena.'

'Hullo Paul. How are you?' She spoke slowly and shyly.

'I'm ... very well thank you very much,' he replied in the formal tone he reserved for adults.

His granny came across to him, pulled up the covers on his bed and arranged them neatly around his chest.

'Feeling better darling?'

'Umph,' he said. He was feeling better but he was not going to admit it. He liked being looked after. He liked his granny endlessly tucking him into bed. He liked her changing his sheets every other day whilst he stood on the cold linoleum feeling weak and strange, and then slipping between them cool and crisp. He liked his meals being brought up to him three times a day: a brown hen's egg for

101

breakfast; ham or lamb for lunch and tinned mandarins or peaches afterwards; brown bread with amber apple jelly and Primula processed cheese for tea. He liked the fruit and the Lucozade all day long. Yes. He would pretend he was still bad for a little while longer.

He sat up in bed and granny plumped his pillows. 'Come over, Philomena,' she called. 'He won't bite! You won't bite, will you?'

'No.'

Settling back on the swollen, cool pillows, he watched his cousin creep across the floor, her sandals sticking to the linoleum and making little soughing noises as she came. Her head was forward, her eyes were hidden.

'Come right up.'

Philomena reached the bed and stood there with her arms by her sides. He glanced quickly at her face and she glanced quickly at him, revealing a row of white teeth behind her slightly moist lips. With her fingers she was worrying the hem of her cardigan. Did she remember? he wondered, the events amidst the copper beeches? He searched her face for a clue but there was none to be read there. None that he was able to see, anyway.

'That's a very pretty jumper.'

'Do you like it Mrs O'Berne?'

'Where did you get it?'

'My mother made it.'

'Wasn't your mammy good. It must have taken her a long while.' Granny moved off towards the door. 'Well, I'm going to leave you two. Will you be all right Pauly?'

She had begun to use the endearment since the accident and his taking to his bed.

'Yes,' he mumbled quietly, blushing and wishing the word could be unsaid.

'You'll be nurse and look after him for a while, Philomena?'

'I will of course.'

'It's down the hall if you want "it" Philomena, through the doors at the end. And perhaps later, Paul, you'll be strong enough to get up.'

'Maybe.'

Granny smiled and closed the door after herself. Her footsteps receded along the hall and down the stairs.

'Are you sick?' asked Philomena.

He nodded and dimly hoped it would not be the usual round of questions.

102

'I was told you fell off a cart.'

'A horse stood on my head, or kicked me on the head I should say.'

'How did that happen?'

'You mustn't tell.'

'I won't.'

'I swore I wouldn't tell. They don't want my father to find out.'

'Would he be cross?'

'He'd be very cross and he'd probably take me away.'

'I won't tell. Cross my heart and hope to die. Promise.'

She spoke emphatically and looked at him with wide blue eyes. Her face was round and white and her blond hair hung down in a single pony-tail. At the front of her head waved a red bow and pinned to her caridgan was a jewelled brooch in the shape of a Celtic cross.

'I brought tea up to the men who were cutting the hay and as a treat they said I could ride back on the cart,' he explained. 'I climbed right up on top of the hay and we began to come back. Joseph was driving. We went down the field and turned into the Bog Road which leads to the yard. Suddenly the horse began to bolt. He was stung by a hornet, Joseph said. I slipped off the rick and fell between the horse and the stays. Then the horse went round a sharp bend and snapped his tackle and that was when I got kicked on the head. But you're not to tell anyone this!'

Philomena shook her head and put a finger to her lips.

'Did it hurt?'

'I don't really remember what happened.'

'I imagine it must have.'

He shrugged his shoulders. It was impossible to say. When he thought back on what had happened it seemed like a dream in which he watched himself participating from a great distance.

'Did you cry?'

'I don't know.'

'You were very brave?'

He shrugged again.

'I'm sure you were very brave. And I'm sure you didn't cry.'

He fiddled with the drawstring of the blind by the bed, running the wooden spindle up and down the cord. Where it joined the roller the string was frayed and it looked to him as though it was going to come away at any moment.

'Can I sit?'

She moved towards the end of his bed.

103

'Of course you can.'

As she settled down the springs creaked embarrassingly. He felt his mind wandering to the afternoon amidst the copper beeches, but put the thought out of his head immediately.

'We had a girl at school,' began Philomena, 'and she died. She was called Joanna Cassidy.'

She turned around so that she was facing him.

'... Her father was a solicitor. She got sick. The teacher called it bone marrow disease or cancer. She got lighter and lighter. Boys could practically lift her up with one hand. She was like a feather. One day she didn't come to school and not long after she died. But the really strange thing was before she died. We were in the playground and Miss O'Hanlon blew the whistle for us to line up in rows for assembly and suddenly this stuff started coming out of Joanna Cassidy's nose, all this yellow stuff. Ugh! It'd make you sick, the sight of it.'

'What was it?'

'It was like egg.'

'Was it like a runny nose?'

'I don't know what it was but it was horrible.'

'There was a boy at my school who died. He was called Teddy Terrington. He died of a hole-in-the-heart. He was very pale, very white, and he wasn't allowed to run or take gym or anything. One day he was late for somewhere. He ran for the bus and that was it. Our form mistress said that everyone in the class had to write to his parents. I didn't know what to write and I went and asked my mother. As she was copying it down she started crying. I asked her what the matter was but she wouldn't say. She just went on crying. After they got the letters Mr and Mrs Terrington wrote back to everyone in the class.'

He released the blind, felt it tug upwards and pulled it down again. How well he remembered it. . . . He and his mother had gone into the cold, cheerless living room at the back of the London house. The green and blue tiles on the floor laid by his father during a DIY spate had been cold. A draught had been coming through the French windows at the end of the room despite the rolled blanket lying along the bottom on the floor. Outside had been their garden and all the other suburban gardens, and fog had slowly been falling on them, the sort that made everything damp. In the windows of the houses lights had glimmered and in the kitchen opposite he had glimpsed Mrs Pritchard bent over her stove. His mother had given him a cup of milk and, because his father had been away, he had been allowed to put in white sugar which normally he had been forbidden. He had sat down at the table and begun to sip the sweet, slightly warm milk. His mother had sat beside him and opened the pad of blue Basildon Bond which she always used for letters. 'Dear Mr and Mrs Terrington,' she had written, 'I was very saddened to hear about the death of your son Teddy as were every one of us in Mrs Harris's class. Teddy was a very popular schoolboy, noted for his zest and enthusiasm, and he made an enormous contribution to the life of the class. . . .'

At that point she had put down her pen and started to shake.

'What's the matter?' he had asked.

She had begun to sob, her body jerking on the seat.

'I'm getting tears on the letter,' she had said.

Tears had indeed fallen on the paper. Where they had landed the paper had bubbled up.

He had persisted with his questions. She had shooed him away. How well he remembered the backs of her hands. He had gone out to the kitchen and had stood there wondering what to do. A moment later she had run after him and put her arms around him.

'I don't want anything to ever happen to you,' she had said and hugged him. Her tears had run down his neck, hot and moist. . . .

'Have you ever seen a dead body?' asked Philomena, interrupting his thoughts.

'Yes.'

'Who did you see?'

'I saw my mother.'

'Was she very beautiful?'

'She looked like she always did.'

'Women are more beautiful in death. Everyone knows that.'

He did not, but he said nothing.

'Did you touch her body?'

He nodded.

'Whereabouts?'

'On the foot in the hospital. Then on the hand in the coffin.'

'Did you touch her face?'

'No I didn't.'

'Was she cold?'

'I knew she was cold, but she didn't feel cold. She felt different.'

'Was it like touching a chicken?'

'It wasn't like anything.'

'Were you frightened?'

'No.'

'Did you think she might sit up?'

'No.'

'They do you know. In the morgue corpses sit up because of the gases in the stomach. My uncle works in a hospital. He told me.'

'Oh.'

'I touched my granny when she died. First I touched her on the foot. . . .'

Philomena point at the sole.

' . . . And there were all these little blue veins on her ankles. Then I touched her neck, her hair, and her forehead. Her skin was all wrinkly and ugh! but underneath she was hard. She was just like a chicken.'

'Do you miss your granny?'

'I did but I don't think of her as much as I used to. Do you miss your mother?'

'I do.'

'I imagine you'd miss a mother more than a granny.'

'I don't know.'

The fell silent. Philomena swung her feet back and forth, the clasps jingling.

'After my granny died,' began Philomena, 'we went to this spiritualist meeting; I mean I went with my parents and a man came out on stage and pointed at me. Then he put his hands over his eyes like this. . . .'

Philomena put her hands over her face.

' . . . He went into a trance. "You've recently had a death in the family," he said and he described my granny. He described exactly what she looked like. He said she was in heaven and she was feeding the chickens and she was all right. He said she often thought about me and she wanted me to know I would be all right. Later the man did hypnotism and I volunteered to go on stage. My mother brought me up and I was hypnotised. The man said I was a very good subject.'

'How did he do it?'

'He had a pendulum on the end of a piece of chain. He told me to concentrate on it, and to think of nothing else. I stared at it going backwards and forwards and he told me to put all my thoughts out of my mind and then he spoke to me.'

'What did he say?'

'I can't remember exactly.'

'Well more or less.'

'He told me to imagine I was floating in the sky. I was floating amongst the clouds, he said, moving here and there like a leaf. Then he told me to imagine that my house was below me and that I was to look down and see it, way below me like a tiny little pin-point. . . .'

Philomena's speech began to slur and her lids to sink. Paul felt vaguely excited. He snapped the cord from the venetian blind and began to swing the spindle from side to side in front of her.

'You're floating in the sky way above your house,' he said. 'You're amongst the clouds, moving here and there like a feather. . . .'

'Like a feather,' she echoed.

'And down below you see your house, very, very small, don't you?'

'I see it, yes! It's in the fields. Our white house in the green fields. I can see the kitchen garden at the back; someone is digging potatoes. I can see the cattle walking towards the cattle trough in a bunch. I can see the chickens around the run, pecking in the grass. I can see our dogs lying in the yard, our two black dogs. I can see everything.'

'And what happens then?'

'I'm floating. I float down ever so slowly.'

'You float down like a feather.'

'I float down, slowly, slowly, slowly, and then I land on the roof of our house.'

Philomena's head was drooping as if her neck could not longer support the weight. Paul felt his excitement growing stronger.

'You land on the roof of your house.'

'I land on the roof. Then I lie back. The sun is shining. I feel the sun on my face. I begin to feel warm all over.'

'And then.'

'Then I begin to feel tired. I feel so tired I want my bed. I want to be warm in my bed.'

'You want to be warm in your bed. Warm and safe.'

'Then the roof parts, it just glides aside and my bedroom is directly underneath and I see my bed. My lovely, warm, soft bed. . . .'

Philomena's voice was slurring more and more, her eyelids lowering, her head drooping.

' . . . I float down and I land on my bed. It's like landing on a huge pile of soft feathers. The blankets and the sheets roll over me and I feel completely. . . . '

Philomena's voice trailed away and her eyes seemed to cloud over.

' . . . You feel completely safe.'

He dropped his hands down and began to study her face. It was round and pale with wisps of blond hair falling over the ears and her forehead. Her lids were half-down, the skin very pale and the eyes seeming not to see. Her lips were red; redder than his. She was breathing gently. Her hands lay neatly on her lap. Her chest rose and fell with regular movements. He unwound the string of the venetian blind from his fingers and dropped it down the side of the bed. The spindle hit the linoleum with a dull noise.

'Are you asleep Philomena?'

'No,' she replied.

'Where are you?'

'I'm in bed at home.'

'Take your shoes off, Philomena,' he whispered.

She undid the clasps and dropped them, one after the other, the clasps jingling as they hit the ground.

'Take your socks off.'

The white ankle socks dropped to the ground and he saw the manufacturer's trade name printed in black along the soles.

'Come here Philomena.'

Philomena climbed down from the bed and trod towards him, her feet sticking to the floor with each step.

'Where are you, Philomena?'

'I'm at home.'

'Where at home?'

'I'm in my bed.'

In his mouth he felt dry. He swallowed and ran his tongue over his teeth.

'Take off your cardigan,' he said very quietly.

Philomena withdrew her arms and it fell to the gound. He strained his ears for sounds of what was happening downstairs. A thump drifted up. It was hard to tell. Perhaps the kettle being put on the Aga. There was a sound of pipes knocking together. Probably granny at the sink. His stomach felt agitated. He lifted back the blankets and shifted over in the bed.

'Come and sit beside me,' he said.

Philomena sat on the edge of the bed.

'Get right in.'

108

She swung her legs onto the bed and put her feet under the
sheets. As she wriggled down he pulled the covers over her.

'Where are you?'

Philomena settled back on the pillow. 'In bed at home.'

'Is it nice?'

'It's safe and warm.'

'Have you just been floating in the sky?'

'Yes.'

He rolled his body towards her and laid his thighs on hers.
Through his pyjamas her skin felt deliciously cool.

'Are you still in bed?'

'Mmh!' she said.

'Close your eyes.'

He stared at her face, watching her lids sink down.

'Eyes closed?'

'Mmh.'

He rolled his body on top of her and lay half-resting on her, half
resting on his elbows and knees. His heart was beating. He thought
it was going to burst out of his chest. Her hair smelt of shampoo and
her skin smelt of soap. It was very white with just a touch of red on
the cheeks. Her eyelashes were short and fair and there were
surprisingly few of them. He brought his mouth to her ear and felt
the warmth of her skin against his lips.

'Are you still asleep?'

'Yes,' she whispered.

His elbows and knees were beginning to ache. Hardly daring to
breathe, he lowered his whole weight onto her. As his middle
touched hers, he felt a surge of excitement.

Shifting slightly to the side, he dropped his leg between Philomena's and began to gently press each way. When the space was
wide enough he dropped between them. His secret part pressed
against hers and he felt something he had never felt before. He
pressed harder. The feeling of pleasure increased. He wanted to be
closer against her. He lifted her dress and pulled it upwards. It was
caught underneath her. It had never been like this when he had
imagined it. He rolled off.

'Still asleep?'

'Yes.'

'Lift your middle up.'

She lifted her torso. He pulled her dress up so that it was above
her middle. She was wearing white knickers. If he took them off
and he took off his pyjamas and he lay back on top of her then he

109

would be doing what his parents had done and what his grandfather had talked about. The mystery would be resolved. He strained his ears. The house was quiet. The principal sound was Philomena's regular breathing.

'Take off ... take off these,' he whispered and pulled at her underwear.

She pulled them off and dropped them on the floor. Her secret place was white and pink; the colour of shell and smooth stone. Here and there, small dark hairs had begun to grow.

He undid the cord of his pyjamas and kicked them away. Philomena breathed quietly. He rolled over and dropped himself between her legs. As his skin touched hers the excitement came back. He pressed and the feeling of pleasure began to come. He pressed harder and dropped his face onto Philomena's hair spread on the pillow. The hair, the shampoo smell, the pillow, he felt excitement rising, rising and rising.

The feeling reached its pitch and broke and he felt there was some sort of moisture between them, between their secret places. Or was it in their secret places? He could not think. He did not dare look.

All was still when up came the sound of the door scraping open. He lifted his head. From below came the tinkling sound of his granny setting down the tray on the table by the kitchen door. Day after day, lying in bed, he had developed an ear for every nuance that marked the coming of granny and the tray that bore his meals. In a moment he knew would come the scraping sound of granny closing the kitchen door. She would pick up the tray. She would begin to walk along the hall. She would turn. She would climb the stairs. She would reach the top. She would cross the landing. She would stop in front of their bedroom door. . . .

He jumped out of bed picked up Philomena's knickers and threaded them over her feet. The tinkling sound. Granny had picked up the tray. She was walking towards the stairs.

'Lift your middle, Philomena,' he urged.

She lifted her middle drowsily. He pulled her knickers up, over the knees and up to the waist. He noticed then the tell-tale red label sticking out at the front like a mocking tongue. Her knickers were back to front and inside out. The stairs were creaking. No time to do anything about it. He pulled her dress down to her knees.

'Lie down, Philomena.'

She lowered her middle. He wrenched his pyjamas from the bottom of the bed and began to pull them on. He could hear the

110

boards creaking as granny rounded the top of the stairs. He tied the knot in his pyjamas cord and pulled the sheets over Philomena. Granny was approaching the door.

'Philomena, would you open the door?' granny called.

'Hold on granny,' he called back. 'I will.'

'Right, Philomena,' he hissed. He clapped his hands. 'Wake up.'

Her eyelids lifted. 'Where am I? Why am I in bed?'

He ran across to the door and pulled it open to his granny standing there with the tray.

'Why Paul. What are you doing out of bed?'

'I'm the doctor now and Philomena's being the patient for a bit.'

'Is she now! Are you the patient Philomena? Oh dearie me. I hope it's nothing contagious.'

'I've got T.B.'

'T.B.?'

'But it's not fatal.'

'Well you seem to have had a remarkable effect on our Pauly,' she said, carrying the tray forward. 'He's been so poorly but you've got him out of bed.'

Philomena lifted away the water glass and the bottle of Lucozade from the bedside chair with the seat of red string. Granny put down the tray. On the white cloth she had laid out a plate of scones with serrated edges, dark jam in a silver dish, a little spoon sticking out of it with the Limerick coat of arms on the end and blue willow-pattern crockery.

'Well Paul, perhaps you'd like to get up after tea? I think you're a lot better now, wouldn't you say?'

He said nothing.

'What would you say, Philomena?

'We could go out and play.' She looked up at him discreetly from the pillow.

'Yes, it would be nice to get up and go out,' he said.

'And let's let some light in,' said granny. 'Lift up the blind, Philomena.' Granny went towards the other window. 'Oh, there's no cord on it,' she said, noticing Philomena was tugging the roller.

'It came off earlier when we were playing,' said Philomena. 'I think it fell under the bed.'

Paul dropped onto his knees and peered across the dusty gloomy linoleum. After a few moments his eyes adjusted and he saw it lying in the corner, the frayed cord with the spindle on the end.

Crack! went the venetian blinds rolling up above.

'Here it is,' he called.

111

He scooted into the dusty dark place and grasped the cord.

When he emerged, the room was bright with sunlight. It made him blink. After a few moments he noticed that Philomena was distinctly smiling at him from the pillow.

'We will go out afterwards?' she enquired.

'Yes,' he replied.

Chapter Seven

The days were getting shorter and the nights colder, although the sun still beat down all day long. Now the eiderdown had appeared, faithful signal of the coming of autumn. Far from sleep, he reached out and stroked the surface: it was a huge assemblage of silken bubbles sewn together with thick, double-stitches. Up and down them he ran his fingers, tracing figures of eight in the darkness.

On the other side of the room granny swallowed and turned on her side.

'When will grandfather be back?' he asked.

'How would I know?'

'Where is he gone?'

'He's standing the harvesters a drink.'

'He always does that?'

She did not reply.

'Has Joseph gone?'

'He has.'

'Have they gone to the hotel?'

'I would think so.'

'I don't really feel all that sleepy.'

'Yes you do. You were yawning earlier. Close your eyes.'

Paul did as she said and immediately his head was filled with the sound of the alarm-clock ticking. When he had been younger and had come to the Red House for his holidays, the clock had used to stand up at night on granny's bed-side chair and it had frightened him then. The phosphorus-green hands and the numbers around the edge had seemed like the eyes of something evil to him; like some sort of snake or monster. These eyes had watched him in the darkness; they had watched him fall asleep; and they had watched him all night long without blinking or moving.

... One summer when he had been very sick and feverish the monster had crawled out of his home at the back of the clock and slithered up onto the bed. 'When you grow big and fat ... ' the monster had whispered ' ... I will open my mouth wide and bite you around the middle. Your legs will wriggle in the air but no one will be able to save you no matter how hard they tug. Then I will swallow you down into my dark belly and there you will stay for ever and ever. . . .' The monster's forked tongue had been black and swollen, Paul remembered, and its freezing breath had smelt of putrid milk. . . .

He opened his eyes and was glad to see there were no phosphorescent eyes staring at him across the darkness. One of the clock's screw-in legs had been lost earlier that summer and so now it lay on its front.

A car passed in the distance, a sound of promise speaking of places faraway, and the dogs scampered below him, the sharp nails of their paws scratching the concrete of the flag. They were circling the house, warding off predators natural and unnatural. He began to feel himself slipping towards sleep. It was a slow movement, like edging down a shelving beach into the sea. . . . Step by step he went, the sea gradually creeping up his body; at last he was up to his waist in it; he sank into the water and began to swim. . . .

There was a cry in the darkness.

'What was that?' Granny sat bolt upright in bed.

Paul opened his eyes. He had heard something, but he could not say; he had been half-asleep.

' . . . I don't know what it is. . . .'

'There's someone out there,' she said. 'Listen. . . .'

'Jesus!' came a voice from the darkness, sudden and terrifying like the cry of someone during a nightmare; then it was quiet again as if the blackness outside had closed round the noise like water. Paul lay still, waiting. But instead of further noises there was a silence so complete he began to wonder if he had not been hearing things. He started to breathe shallowly, fearing his own respiration might prevent him hearing. The clock ticked. There was nothing and then, quite distinctly, came the rasp of a metal barrel being clumsily drawn back.

'They're at the front gate,' he whispered.

As the gate juddered open on its rusty hinges, someone or something fell flatly and there was a peel of laughter.

'Help me up here,' laughed a voice.

'Oh my God!' said granny.

She threw back the covers and leapt out of bed.

'God help us and preserve us.' She turned on the light.

He watched by the yellowish sickly glow of the bulb, as she hurriedly pulled on her cream-coloured dressing gown. Her hair was plaited at the back but a few lengths had come free and stuck out like coiled wires.

114

Underneath the window beside him, where the dogs had scampered a moment before, feet shuffled unsteadily on the concrete flag and a quiet voice spoke that was different to the first voice Paul had heard.

'Nearly there ... ' muttered the quiet voice, ' ... just a few steps. ...'

As granny left the room he swung himself out of bed and fished for his slippers. His granny had not asked him to come with her and when he followed after her, as he intended to, she might try and send him back. But he would not go back, he decided: he would stand by her.

The kitchen window banged below. Paul stood up and removed his hanky from his pyjama pocket. He always took a hanky to bed but he did not like to be seen with it. It gave the impression of an unmanly breast. A series of metallic sounds fluttered up. As he put his arms into his dressing gown he calculated that the key was being taken from its hiding place under the enamel soap-dish by the sink. There was a clatter of something large and hard falling to the floor. The lid! he thought. Beyond the bedroom door he saw granny standing on the landing by the orange-coloured set of glass steps which they used for displaying vases of flowers. She smoothed her hair back from her forehead. Her face was pale. He gave his dressing-gown cord a last tug and moved quietly towards her.

Granny went down the stairs one by one, her head bent forward. He followed discreetly behind, his eyes fixed on the swinging hem of her night-dress. Thump! came the particular sound of the back door knocking the kitchen wall and the latch digging into the hole which had been hollowed there in the plaster by years of daily banging. They stopped to listen, each holding the cold, sticky bannister.

'Turn on the blasted electric light ... ' slurred a voice.

The stiff bakelite switch resounded like a distant pistol shot.

'Turn on all the lights ... ' continued the voice.

When he had heard the cry in the darkness before, Paul had pretended it was not who it was. But now there could be no doubt about it. It was grandfather and he was drunk.

'Isn't it a waste to turn all the lights on?' asked the other, quieter one.

'Turn them all on! grandfather shouted back.

The switches for the scullery, the pantry and the back-kitchen clicked on, like a fusillade of shots at an execution.

Granny began to descend again, he following after. As his feet

115

touched the hall tiles, the door leading from the kitchen swung open.

' . . . Turn them lights all bloody on and we'll blaze through the whole country . . . ' shouted grandfather as he staggered through, supported at the shoulder by Joseph.

'What in the name of God is going on?' asked granny quietly, stepping in front of them.

She halted below the hallway light with the glass shade full of dead flies, which consequently cast a strange, mottled pattern of light and shadow.

'Hello Mrs O'Berne . . . ' slurred Joseph.

He blinked nervously and looked at her through his slightly misted-up spectacles. His sausage-skin complexion was flushed red and gleamed like a polished tile. Grandfather hung beside him like a balloon filled with water, his head tilting at an alarming angle.

'Once more you have disgraced yourself. Once more you have broken your word,' said granny. 'I'll never believe you again.'

'Pah!' Grandfather drew himself up as if he were about to shout.

'What happened?' asked granny.

On the side of his head which had been lolling against Joseph's shoulder, there was a cut shaped like a wriggling serpent. Half-congealed blood with the consistency of a soft-boiled egg was matted into the hair around it.

'We had a little fall,' replied Joseph sheepishly. 'No bones broken though.' He waggled grandfather's limp body to prove his point.

Granny took her husband by his free arm and she and Joseph began to climb the stairs. It was a slow process. At the third step, grandfather dropped his head back and began to sing:

' . . . Her eyes they sh - one like dia - monds you'd think she was queen - of the land. . . . '

Standing numb in the hallway, watching and listening, Paul suddenly noticed the strong smell of dung. He looked down and saw that it was smeared all over the tiles, from the kitchen door to the bottom of the stairs. He did not have to think where it had come from.

He glanced upwards, pointlessly he knew, and saw that the dung was stuck to grandfather's and Joseph's shoes like clogged mud. It was a moist dung on account of the rich, late-summer grass which the cows were eating, and pungent to the nose.

He closed his eyes. 'I will not be sick. I will not be sick . . . ' he recited inwardly.

116

'. . . As I walked down the Broadway, not intending to stay very long . . . ' sang grandfather.

There was a crash but Paul paid no attention to it.

A moment later his granny called to him: 'Paul,' she shouted crossly, 'come and open the door.'

He began to climb the stairs with his lips firmly pressed together, taking care to avoid the dark blobs on the carpet. The idea of the smell of the green stuff in his mouth was almost unbearable.

On the floor of the landing halfway up lay the photograph of the American girl and her horse in the field of white flowers. The frame was broken and the glass was shattered. Once it had been his favourite picture but now he hardly noticed it.

'. . . I met with a pretty young cailin . . . ' murmured grandfather.

He ran up the remaining stairs and opened grandfather's bedroom door.

'Turn on the light,' said granny.

He found the switch in the darkness and turned it on.

'. . . Her eyes they sho - ne like dia - monds . . . '

Grandfather's single bed lay along the wall opposite the door. Granny and Joseph manoeuvred him over and then let go of him. His body flopped onto the bed and the mattress bounced and squeaked.

'Help a decent man to a smoke,' called grandfather, fumbling at one of his pockets.

'Yes boss' replied Joseph with an imbecilic grin.

But before he could step forward, granny had taken his arm.

'Go downstairs,' she said, 'and put on the kettle.'

At the sound of her cold, tired voice, the smirk vanished from Joseph's face. He began to look ashamed.

'I'm sorry for all the trouble I've caused you,' he whined.

'Yes, yes. Now go down to the kitchen. I'll be along in a minute.'

'I want a fag,' called grandfather.

'Yes James. When I've got you into bed you can have a fag.'

She lifted up her husband's legs hanging over the side of the bed and saw for the first time that his boots were mired.

'Oh no,' she said quietly, and removed them without dirtying her hands.

'Go and put them in the bucket in the bathroom,' she said, handing them to Paul when she had finished.

He carried the shoes out by their tongues as if they were danger-ous animals. He saw the mire was dark green, something like spinach, and he guessed that it had oozed into all the little holes that

117

decorated the uppers. He did not study it closely as he knew it would make him sick.

Reaching the side of the enamel bath, he peered into the bucket that stood inside it.

'It's full of clothes,' he wailed.

Wildly, he looked around for somewhere to put the shoes but there was nowhere suitable. There was not even a newspaper lying around to lie them on.

'The bucket's full,' he cried again.

Granny rushed in behind him.

'The one time I need your help and you start acting the fool,' she exclaimed, taking a cloth from the S-bend under the sink.

'Just tip the bucket and put the shoes in it.' She ran out.

'Holding the shoes with one hand, Paul reached into the soapy, scummy mixture with the other. The submerged clothes felt slithery and oily. He lifted them out of the water and held them dripping over the bucket. The tangled mixture included grandfather's long-johns, noticeably darker at the crotch, socks with elastic supports, and various unnameable items of feminine underwear.

' . . . What about now? What about now woman? Strip off and jump in . . . ' he heard his grandfather calling.

Water drops like falling rain pattered in the bath. Oh please, let this be over soon! he thought.

' . . . Come on James, lift your arm . . . ' urged granny.

He heaved the sopping bundle into the sink, repeating the draining process twice more and the bucket was empty.

' . . . Come on . . . ' grandfather's voice floated in; ' . . . a quick in and out! It won't take long. . . . '

He tipped the bucket into the bath that was like pumice stone to touch. The washing water was filthy grey and full of flecks, especially wollen bits from the socks. He turned on the cold tap, gave the bucket a rinse and dropped the shoes in with a dull clang.

' . . . You're bloody useless as a woman . . . ' came a cry.

His left hand was covered with a dirty, suddy film and granules of detergent.

' . . . That's a nice way to talk . . . ' replied granny.

He rinsed his hand and turned the tap off, then half-dried it on the hem of his dressing gown, The fabric chafed and made his skin red.

He left the bathroom and clumped across the landing. He wanted to announce his coming.

'I did what you said with the shoes,' he called ahead of himself into the bedroom.

'Good boy.' Her voice was mechanical.

She was bent over the bed folding back the counterpane. The bedding hung over grandfather's thin body like a tent stretched over a taut wire.

He clicked his fingers.

'I want that fag,' he demanded.

'Paul, fetch your grandfather a cigarette,' said granny walking towards the door with his mired trousers.

'I'll make some tea and some bread and butter, James.'

As she walked out of the door, grandfather stared after her with large, grey, angry eyes. An eternity seemed to pass.

'Where are the cigarettes?' Paul finally asked in his most timid tones.

'In the blasted pocket.'

He fished in the jacket hanging over the chair and pulled out twenty cellophane-wrapped 'Gold Flake' cigarettes, a white packet with a stripe down the front. He was being watched, he could feel it.

'You love your grandfather most, don't you?' he heard.

Of all the questions that he dreaded this was the one he dreaded the most. He turned towards the mantelpiece where the ashtray and the matches were sitting.

'Yes I do.' He presented his back, hoping this would hide his lack of conviction.

He rattled the box to make certain it was not empty and picked up the ashtray. It was shaped like a horse-shoe with a picture of a mare nuzzling a foal on the china bottom.

'Nearly there,' he said in the way which he believed was adultlike and soothing.

As he crossed the room, little flecks of grey flew out of the ashtray onto his hand and he smelt the distinctive odour of old cigarettes. It was the smell which, more than any other, he connected with his grandfather.

He stopped by the bed. Grandfather was a rod under the sheets.

'Here they are,' he said.

'Open them.'

As he began to separate the cellophone halves, he felt grandfather's eyes staring at him. His skin felt funny. He took a sidelong glance. Old fears began to stir, dating from the era of the clock and the phosphorescent eyes. There was a serpent inside grandfather; it was a thin, wiry serpent, like his thin wiry body. The serpent hid behind grandfather's face and looked out through grandfather's eyes. His cold trunk trailed down grandfather's throat and coiled up

119

in grandfather's stomach. The slight swell in his old man's belly was the serpent's body pushing outwards. The serpent was waiting for the right moment and, when it came, he was going to leap out through grandfather's mouth and devour everyone in sight, starting with himself. . . .

'Have you ever had a smoke?'

The cellophane suddenly came away.

'No . . . no I've never. . . .'

He pushed up the cardboard drawer and removed the silver paper covering the cigarettes.

'They're coffin nails.' Grandfather took one of the slim white cylinders and put it between his lips.

'What shall I do with this?' asked Paul, crumpling up the cellophane and the silver paper.

'Put it in the ashtray you fool.'

Grandfather began to fumble in the matchbox. His eyelids trembled like the wings of an insect in the wind.

After a painful number of attempts he at last managed to extract a match.

'Would you like me to light it for you?' Paul asked politely, his voice so low it was almost inaudible.

'I'm not an invalid. I can do it myself,' grandfather barked back.

It was always his way, to return a gentleness with a blow! Paul thought.

Grandfather drew the match along the sandpaper several times. The match-end sparked and finally spluttered alight. He held it for a few seconds, allowing the flame to spread along the wood, then lifted it with two hands to the end of the cigarette. The tobacco caught fire and glowed. Smoke that was almost blue came out of the side of his mouth.

He swung the match back and forth through the air but the flame, instead of dying, grew bigger. He dropped it burning into the horse-shoe. The crumpled cellophane shivered with the heat and a tiny glowing circle began to grow on one side. Paul watched it nervously as it grew bigger, the match flaming close by.

'It's on fire.' He pointed at the ashtray.

Grandfather did not appear to hear him. He touched the cut on the side of his head and stared at the blood on his finger tips.

'I hurt myself,' he said.

The silver paper was beginning to burn. Paul could not stand still any longer. He bent forward and huffed at the ashtray. Flecks of material rose into the air.

120

'Leave it alone can't you! It'll burn out in its own time. Bring up the tea.'

Ash that was the colour of city snow drifted down and landed silently on the white pillow.

'I'll be back up in a moment then.'

Grandfather nodded and took another puff.

Paul turned round and crossed the room. As he closed the door, the last thing he saw was grandfather lying in bed with his eyes closed, the white cigarette dangling from his lips and the horse-shoe resting on his belly. Low flames showed above the rim and a little smoke drifted upwards, reminding him of his favourite indoor firework, 'Mount Vesuvius'.

Coming towards the kitchen he heard Joseph inside.

'I'm sorry. I'm really sorry,' said the hand.

Paul pushed open the door. Joseph sat at the table blinking behind his still partially misted spectacles. An old local newspaper taken from the pile in the scullery lay on the floor beside him.

'Tell me what happened.'

Granny stood at the Aga with her back to him. Though Paul could not see, he knew she was staring with small, dark eyes at the aluminium kettle sighing in front of her.

'He didn't have a drink all evening,' began Joseph slowly. 'It was lemonade every time. And then this fellow came up to him and he says, "You'll have a drink;" and the boss says, "I will not. I'll have a lemonade." And the fellow says, "You'll have a drink surely? To keep us company?" And the boss says, "I'll take a sherry then." So I said, "But you mustn't boss," and the boss says, "I'm only taking it out of politeness; don't you see that?" You see he was only taking it out of politeness.'

'Go on.'

'He asked for a sherry in a small glass. At that stage he wasn't serious you see. The sherry came and he drank it down. His eyes got bigger and he started to shake. He called for a brandy. I said, "Boss, don't mix it." But he wouldn't listen. The brandy came. He drank the bottle off. Then he started on a second. He began to get rowdy. The hotel said they were closing and that was when I brought him back.'

'Who offered him the sherry?'

'I don't remember.'

'What did he look like?'

'I can't remember. A big man.'

'What was his name?'

121

'I don't remember.'

'Take off your boots Joseph.'

'Oh yes. Sorry Mrs O'Berne. Will I put them on the paper?'

'Where else?'

He bent down and began to undo his boot laces. The leather threads pulling through the eyes slapped against the uppers, making a queer clack-clack sound like knitting needles.

'Why didn't you prevent him?'

'I tried.'

'You tried! You should have insisted. You of all people. You know the consequences.'

'You don't know what he's like. He'd go berserk. He'd smash you in two.'

'I know very well what he's like and I'd have taken the bottle from him.'

The lid on the kettle began to float in the steam, tapping on the rim like a branch knocking against a window.

'I'm ashamed of you Joseph. You should have stopped him.'

She measured the tea brusquely and then threw the spoon back in the caddy with a clang. Carelessly she poured in the water and droplets spattered on the hot ring and hissed. At the finish she slammed on the lid of the tea-pot.

'I'm sorry,' said Joseph again. His second boot was off. He wore no socks. He wriggled his toes. The edges of his nails were filthy black.

'Sorry's no good when you don't have to contend with him.'

There was a painful silence as she poured the tea. Joseph dropped his head and made a little gasping sound as though he were about to cry.

'Paul.' She pronounced his name wearily.

He sprang across the kitchen with an eagerness which he hoped would please and pacify her.

'Bring these up to your grandfather.' She held out a cup with a saucer balanced on top to keep in the heat and a side-plate with two pieces of buttered shop-bread on it.

As he took them Paul looked into her eyes with his most consoling expression. From the look that she returned he knew that she had seen, but the acknowledgement and gratitude which he had hoped for did not follow. Instead she turned away and asked Joseph if he wanted tea. His mother would never have done this! he thought as he slipped out the door.

Carefully avoiding the green, drying blobs with a crust on the outside, he began to climb the stairs.

122

His mother's eyes had always been grey, he remembered, when she had been sad but when he had looked into them they had always lightened up. It had been like sunshine after rain when that happened. With granny it seemed it was different. He recalled her face in the kitchen, so set and so defeated and it occurred to him dimly that there were some pains which were beyond consolation.

There was a smell like burnt sugar. He stopped and sniffed the air. Strange it was. The wind was howling, hugging its belly to the tiles as it coursed over the roof. He felt a strange prickly sensation between his shoulder blades. His thoughts of mother and granny vanished.

He resumed his climb. He went slowly. He was apprehensive. His slippers seemed to crash on the carpet. Something was odd. The smell did not seem to be exactly the smell of burnt sugar and the wind seemed to be more inside than outside. He shivered. He wanted to turn round and go down. He was being ridiculous, he told himself.

'The king was in his counting house, counting out his money, the queen was in her parlour, eating bread and honey,' he recited. And granny was in the kitchen with Joseph and grandfather was in his bedroom.

He reached grandfather's door. There was still time to turn round and flee. But that was absurd. He noticed there was something funny about the door. He bent forward. Here and there on the wooden panels there were little liquid droplets. It was as if the door were sweating or weeping.

There is something in there! he thought. His heart began to beat. He was behaving like a baby, he told himself. His heart beat faster. There *was* something in there. He knew there was something in there. And he knew what it was. The monster was in there. He was curled up inside grandfather's belly, with his head at the back of grandfather's throat and he was waiting, Paul knew he was waiting for himself.

He put down the tea and side-plate on the stairs and knocked on the wood.

'Grandfather?' he called palely. He noticed the wood was slightly warm. The wind moaned more loudly. It was the monster squirming inside. It was waiting to jump out at him.

He had known this moment once before when he had seen the school bullies waiting outside the school gates. As he had walked towards them – they were not waiting particularly for him but for anyone small and vulnerable – he had wondered if he should not turn back and seek the protection of a teacher. But that idea had filled him with even greater fear than had the certain knowledge of the beating which lay ahead. If he had turned back then he would have failed himself in a way that could never have been put right again, and similarly he knew that if he turned back from grandfather's door, he would regret it forever afterwards.

He reached for the handle and it was hot. He withdrew his arm into his sleeve and used the cuff as a glove. He slowly turned the handle. It was now or never. There was no going back.

He pushed the door open and a huge red and yellow flame jumped out at him, like a Jack-in-the-box. He jumped back in terror, knocking over the tea-cup.

'Granny' he called. Dimly he was aware of hot tea running over his foot.

The room was a red and yellow box of fire with flames clinging to everything like *aurora borealis* on the rigging of a ship. The yellow shag carpet in front of the fire-place was alight; the yellowing, speckled blind, its cord and the wooden weight at the bottom with the rubber band around it were alight; the mildewed, coppery wallpaper and the border of roses at the top were alight; the plastic holy water font above the bedhead was alight, its brown form melting in the heat and sliding like treacle down the wall; the green and white candlewick bedspread was alight: the swollen white bolster was alight; and so also, quite still in the middle of the raging flames, was the figure lying on the fiery bed with his back to Paul.

'Grandfather,' called Paul, but all that he heard was the noise of the flames.

He stepped forward and immediately ran into a wall of intense heat in the doorway. He felt it first in his eye-balls. He felt as if someone had poked their fingers into them. Then he felt it on his face. He felt his cheeks getting very hot very quickly. It was not like burning oneself or touching a scalding plate. It was more than that. The pale thin skin of his face was being scorched. He put his hands to his cheeks.

He saw that flames were running towards him. It was like the movement of rats scuttling in the undergrowth. It was fast, it was unstoppable and by being close to the ground it turned the strength he had that came from height into a vulnerability and a weakness. He stepped back.

'Granny,' he called again.

The carpet that ran along the centre of the landing was alight at the edges and the lino underneath was beginning to blister. So was the paint on the door and the door frame. It rose in bubbles that were like the bumps in dough that has stood for hours. The curtain at the end of the landing caught from the carpet, the flames climbing easily with rapid movements like a monkey in a cage. Then the dried flowers on the stand close by caught with a whoosh. Within a moment the whole bunch was alight and crackling like stubble in a field. The glass vase which held them cracked in two and the burning flowers fell slowly sideways. As they hit the floor they disintegrated and small burning wisps were thrown upwards and began to float through the air like the seeds of a dandelion. He felt strangely light-headed and impervious to the dangers around him. He stared at the burning flakes. How beautiful they were. And how beautiful suddenly everything was. . . .

'Oh my God,' he heard granny saying behind him. He turned and saw her. Her skin was white.

Joseph was beside her. His glasses had slipped down his nose and he was looking over the upper rims at what was happening. His eyes were small and his expression was sheepish.

Suddenly Joseph began to lurch towards the flaming doorway.

'Stop him for God's sake,' called granny.

Paul watched Joseph coming towards him. With his arms folded over his head like a paper hat in a children's story book, he struck Paul as comical. It also occurred to him that Joseph was trying to be brave. He stepped forward. It would be ages before they collided. Then suddenly he felt it: Joseph's knees digging into his legs, Joseph's body thumping against his.

Granny ran up and took Joseph by the side of his coat. Paul grabbed one of his thick wrists with his small boyish hands.

'Come back. You'll never get out if you go in,' his granny shouted.

'Let me go,' Joseph shouted back, trying to barge forward.

'Don't be an idiot.'

'Idiot!' What a strange word, Paul thought, for his granny to use. . . .

Huge flames had started to lick through the door and dark smoke had begun to cloud the atmosphere. He coughed. His lungs were hurting. They felt sooty and dry. His eyes were hurting too. He felt like rubbing them but he did not have the strength to lift his hands to them. It was such a long way to lift them. His knees were sagging. He felt them going. Yes. Rest for a moment or two.

He closed his eyes. There was a bed. It was his bed. The pillow was white and plumped up. It would be cool on his cheeks. The

125

blankets were pulled back. It was only a matter of climbing in. How good at last to be able to rest. He reached out towards it. . . .

'Come on,' his granny called.

He felt his body being moved. He opened his eyes and saw there were now flames behind them where there had been none before. They had spread down the stairs themselves. They would have to go down it as if into a well of fire. Joseph and granny each took him by the hand. There was a large crash and a blinding white flash.

'Let's make a run,' someone said.

Yes! he thought, must make a run. Outside it would be cool; the grass would be wet with dew. He would run through it in his bare feet. He would wet his toes. The wind would fan his cheeks and the uncomfortable hot, burning feeling that he felt would go away. Yes, outside into the cool, night air, that was the place to be.

They began to run down. He felt heat stroking across him, everywhere; stroking across his feet; the backs of his legs; the top of his head. He saw the glass partition at the bottom of the stairs inlaid with glass fleur-de-lys. He was moving but it was not getting any closer. Then suddenly they reached the hall, the tiles still cold through his slippers. They raced across, opened the vestibule door and there it was, big and white, the door that led to the cold fields, the cool grass, the open night sky silvered with stars, a rumpled moon, white and cool, trees with green leaves sighing quietly in the wind.

There was another crash somewhere above. Granny turned the key and, in the absence of any handle, began to heave on it. The door would not budge. Since the snows had swollen the lintel it had never been easy to open.

'You try, Joseph.'

He took hold of the key and began to pull on it.

'No! Joseph. You must turn the key. You must turn the key and pull at the same time!'

Joseph looked at her uncomprehendingly and continued to pull without turning it.

'The kitchen door,' his granny shouted.

They ran back into the hall. It was like diving into a sea of heat. Paul gasped. His throat was melting; his eyes were melting; his skin was melting. The bones beneath felt raw, as if they had been pummelled. It was like someone had hit him with a stick in the face. They had hit him really hard. They had hit him on the eyes and on the throat and on the mouth. They had hit him all over so that he was sore and bruised. Now all that he wanted to do was to close

126

himself between creamy sheets, lay his face on a pillow with a white pillow-slip, feel the cold extremity at the bottom of the bed with his toes and fall fast asleep underneath the heavy comforting weight of blanket piled on blanket.... And when the morning came he would wake to see the sun slanting on the curtains; he would hear the dogs scampering below, their nails scratching on the flag; and he would smell bacon frying in the kitchen downstairs. There was a blinding white flash and he closed his eyes....

The next thing that Paul knew his feet were wet and cold. He looked down at the ground. He was standing in dewy grass. There were odd bits of foliage stuck to his brown furry slippers. The bottoms of his pyjama legs were sodden as well and clung to his ankles.

He shivered and looked up. Ahead of him stood the Red House burning ferociously in the darkness. The flames which leapt towards the sky were huge. They were like the hands of a fallen giant appealing for help. Nearby, the leaves of the copper beech trees reflected the flames and glistened eerily in the darkness with a peculiar sort of mauve colour. They were spectating giants watching the slow death of another as he rolled in agony before them.

There was a crashing noise. Rover and Lassie crouched nearby, whimpered in the darkness. The flames appeared to part like a curtain in the theatre and Paul saw a large black hole where the roof had been. A moment later flames began to lick through the hole, there was another crash, sparks flew out and the flames leapt up again, obscuring everything.

It was then he remembered what had happened. Grandfather was inside lying on his fiery bed with his face turned towards the wall. He was asleep; it was the sleep which, Paul knew, everyone took at the end of their lives; it was the sleep which lasted for ever. Grandfather was asleep and his soul was travelling towards heaven. Was that upwards or downwards? Above the sky or below the earth? He had often tried to gently enquire of its whereabouts but everyone that he had questioned had always been elusive on the subject. They had always said that they could not say exactly and that heaven was not exactly a geographical place. Whenever he had pressed the enquiry, they had always become defensive and, in the end, everyone had always made more or less the same statement: heaven was inside; it was a state of mind. He had never understood this and he still did not understand it. How could it be anything but a proper place? Was it not always drawn as a proper place of clouds and thrones, which was always packed with throngs of people with bare feet? He recalled the picture that had hung in the kitchen of Mary with a white round face and small eyes, sitting amidst crowds, a gold bulbous crown resting on her head. The Assumption of the Blessed Virgin, it had been called. His granny had told him the picture showed the arrival of the Virgin in heaven. As shown in the picture heaven was a place. It was a place where one went. Then, quite suddenly a new and startling thought crossed his mind: perhaps the crash that he had heard had been the sound of grandfather's soul going to heaven.

'Has grandfather gone to heaven?' he asked.

'Yes dear,' his granny said and he felt her touching the back of his head.

Something was troubling him. What was it? It was like a name on the tip of the tongue. It was there, it was almost there. Then he knew what it was. It was his last vision of grandfather lying in his bed, the cigarette wrappings burning in the ashtray that was resting on his middle.

With the picture came the idea that perhaps he, Paul was responsible for what had happened. After all, he had left the papers burning in the ashtray and gone downstairs. He had not put them out which he had known at the time he should have. If anyone found out he would be in the most terrible trouble. Perhaps granny suspected it? Perhaps that was why she sounded far away.

There was another crash inside the house. The flames parted and sparks flew into the darkness like fireflies. This time he was in no doubt as to what was happening: it was the rest of the roof collapsing and the chimney stacks at each end falling after it. The force of the collapse gave him an impression of anger. Perhaps it was grandfather going to heaven angrily. He would be angry, of course, and it would be with Paul that he would be angry. Paul had left the papers burning in the ashtray. Paul had been responsible.

'Has grandfather really gone to heaven?' he asked again.

'Yes,' replied granny but once again her voice sounded faint.

No, he could not be certain from the way that she spoke. It was possible that grandfather's soul had not really gone to heaven. If this was so then the consequences for him could be dire. He remembered hearing once that the dead haunted those that were living if they had a grievance against them. He wondered if this was going to happen to him? He pictured it. On a dark night, from behind a tree or under his bed or from a dark corner at the back of a wardrobe, his grandfather was going to appear. He would be on fire of course and his eyes would be shining like they did when he was drunk. He would take Paul by the hand and Paul would feel his skin blistering until it began to burn and then his whole body would catch and he would burst into flames.

The two of them together would then run from wherever they were, out into the fields. Then they would run through the darkness, across the grass and over walls, through woods and past farms with dogs that barked at them ferociously. They would never stop, once they began; they would never pause for breath; they would run for ever and ever. . . .

Paul's heart began to race; his temples felt hot; and his breathing was shallow as though he had a fever. His lower body in comparison was cold, especially his feet: he stamped them gently.

'Cold feet lovey?' asked granny.

He felt her legs pressing against him and her lips on his neck. She began to stroke the top of his head again.

'Oh Joseph' she said, 'your boots were inside in the kitchen. Your feet must be soaked.'

Joseph's two very white feet looked like strange vegetables lying in the grass.

'I lost my spectacles,' he said with his teeth chattering.

'Where did you lose them?' asked granny.

'I don't remember. I had them inside.'

'Perhaps they're here somewhere.'

The three of them dropped down onto their haunches and ineffectively patted the grass around their feet. They found nothing, only the dew and dock leaves and the odd flat thistle which sharply pricked their skin.

'We won't find them,' said granny straightening up.

'Will I be able to have a new pair?' asked Joseph. He was still squatting on the ground.

'Of course you will.'

'I had them since I was twelve. My mother got them off a man. Will I get another?'

'Of course you will. Of course.'

The gate clanged open at the bottom of the Avenue. Paul turned round and saw that a crowd had gathered just inside the demesne. He had not noticed them come in. He thought he could make out one of the families from the cottages, the Cavanaghs, talking in their low impenetrable accents.

A figure began to advance towards them, shouting and waving in the darkness. The figure was trying to run but had obviously not run for years. Progress was slow and ungainly. It was Mr McKenna. As

129

he drew closer Paul heard something about a fire engine. It had been summoned. It was only a matter of time. Mr McKenna reached their side.

'Where is . . .?' he asked breathlessly before he cut himself short.

'He's above,' said granny pointing aimlessly towards the house.

Mr McKenna began to repeat himself. The fire station had been notified, he said. They were on their way. It was only a matter of time. He spoke in a strange, excited way Paul noticed. It was a way he had never heard Mr McKenna speak before. It was fast and garbled, rather than Mr McKenna's usual crawling brogue. It sounded to him as though Mr McKenna were out of control and might at any moment burst into tears or begin to laugh uncontrollably.

'Perhaps the situation can still be saved, please God,' said Mr McKenna. His hopefulness made Paul wince. A whole new perspective which had something to do with human folly hovered on the edge of his understanding.

Mr McKenna was wheezing and breathless. He took off his hat and rubbed away the sweat that clustered in beads on his temples.

Granny spoke in her faraway voice again. She thanked Mr McKenna for what he had done. He was a good neighbour, she said. But she added that the whole business was hopeless. Nothing was to be saved from the situation.

Mr McKenna tut-tutted and shook his head. 'Never give up hope,' he said. 'Hope springs eternal. We don't know yet and we won't know, so let's not make up our minds yet.'

'Oh I know,' said granny, 'I know.' There was a pause and then she spoke again. 'Have you any shoes spare at home, Mr McKenna? Joseph left his own above in the house.'

'I have,' said Mr McKenna.

Paul watched him as he put his hat back onto his head.

'Are you feeling all right, Mrs O'Berne?' he asked with a peculiar intonation of intimacy. This was a new way of speaking again which Paul had never heard coming from Mr McKenna before.

'Yes Mr McKenna,' said granny, 'I'm all right, thank you very much.'

'Would you like to come down to our house and wait?' he asked.

'No,' she said. 'I'll stay here, I'll wait until the firemen come. I'll wait for a bit anyhow.'

Paul shivered. His slippers were wet right through and he could feel the damp between his toes. He wanted to lie down again; he wanted to go to sleep.

'I'm going to sit down,' he said and pointed at the cluster of trees nearby. One of them had fallen over years before and formed a natural bench.

'You go and sit down, lovey, you must be exhausted. Mr McKenna will bring you down presently. Won't you Mr McKenna?'

'I will,' he said. 'I will of course. I'll bring him now if you like.'

'Would you like to go now, Paul?'

'No,' he said. 'I'd like to sit for a bit.'

As he walked towards the cluster of trees, Paul saw that there were sheep and bullocks huddled underneath the spreading branches. They were staring across the darkness at the burning house, their big eyes glinting red with the flames. As he drew closer they shied away and he heard them retreating through the undergrowth. He reached the fallen tree and sat down. He was so tired. He twisted his body and laid his head on the trunk. The damp, rough wood smelled mossy and cold. It was a smell which reminded him of graveyards and tombstones. Behind him he could hear the animals breathing and stamping. They were frightened and at the same time they wanted to draw closer. He shut his eyes. How nice it would be to be Jesus, he thought. Oh how sweet to sleep in the manger, cosseted in dry, warm straw; the animals around one; the angels above him; and his mother watching over him close by.

There were red shadows on the wooden ceiling cast by the embers of the fire. He lay quite still, watching the flickering movements and listening. McKenna's kitchen was full of strange noises, particularly a strange clicking behind the wainscotting.

He reminded himself that Mrs McKenna was only a few feet away upstairs but it seemed such a distance. Yes, she would hear him if he called out in the darkness but could she come quickly enough? If only granny had been in the house but she had gone with Mr McKenna to break the news to his uncles twenty miles away.

I will not be frightened, he recited inwardly, and grandfather will not return. . . .

He repeated the phrase over and over again in the belief that it would calm him.

Whew! came a sound of terrifying proximity. He sat up in bed. The clock was ticking on the shelf over the fire. The window shivered in the casement. He wanted to whisper, 'Who's there?' but

131

when he opened his mouth he felt no sound could be coaxed from between his lips.

Whew! it came again. It was not outside, he realised, but inside. He was beginning to burn. Remain absolutely still, he told himself. Breathe shallowly. Listen.

Whew! came the noise for the third time. Now there could be no doubt. It was inside his room underneath his makeshift bed.

He stared into the darkness. In the middle was the kitchen table with four chairs set around it. He could see their tall backs glistening like red spears. The light switch was on the far side by the door. If he threw back the covers he could jump onto the floor. Three big steps and the switch would be his.

It was now or never, he told himself. He pushed back the blankets and began to scramble to his feet. There being a danger the serpent would slither out from under the bed and bite his ankles, it was his intention to leap into the middle of the floor. But as he drew himself to full height, the bed tipped backwards and he found himself on the lino with the pillows around his ankles. He kicked free, raced past the table and grasped the switch.

The light clicked on and he braced himself for fight or flight. But instead of the worst he found himself looking down at Mrs Mc-Kenna's cocker spaniel, Didi, a brown and white dog with floppy ears and staring bloodshot eyes. One end of the camp bed rested on the ground and the other jutted into the air like the stern of a sinking ship.

A door above banged open and he heard footsteps on the stairs. A moment later Mrs McKenna appeared beside him, her sturdy form enclosed in a blue quilted dressing gown.

'What happened?'

'Didi was under the bed and I didn't know it was her.'

The old dog waddled forward, wagging her platypus tail.

'Did old Didi give Pauly a fright?'

Mrs McKenna bent down and patted Didi's expectant cranium.

'Naughty, naughty Didi. Say sorry!' Didi took a step towards Paul. 'Good doggy.' Mrs McKenna slowly straightened up. 'You see, Didi's saying she's sorry.'

The disagreeable odour of Didi drifted up as he touched her slightly oily pelt. Along her sides Didi's flesh was thick and rippled.

'I should have told you and I'm sorry that I didn't. Didi always sleeps in here and she snores. Did she give you a terrible fright?'

'I was a bit frightened.'

'You look as white as a sheet.'

She hurried forward and tipped the canvas bed frame back onto the floor.

'Let's get you back into bed. What you need is to sleep.'

She folded back the covers and plumped the pillows into place.

'Come on. In you get.'

He put his feet between the sheets and slid down.

'You know you've nothing to be frightened of.'

She knelt down beside him bringing her face close to his. There was white cream on her cheeks and what hair she had was held in place by a black net.

'Is grandfather angry with me?' he asked quietly.

'No. Of course not. He loved you very much. Why would he be angry with you?'

'Because of the fire.'

'That wasn't your fault. That was an accident. Your grandfather asked for a cigarette. Your granny told you to give him one and went down to make tea. She told us that, do you remember?'

He nodded and swallowed.

'Grandfather was tired. He must have dropped the cigarette or something and the cigarette set fire to his bed.'

At least Mrs McKenna and granny did not suspect he had left the papers burning in the ashtray. There was comfort in that.

'Has grandfather gone to heaven?'

'Of course grandfather has gone to heaven. You don't have to worry about that, my darling.

'How do you know?'

'Because it's the truth.'

'Do people ever come back from heaven?'

'Never.'

'Do they never really come back after they've died?'

'I've never known anyone to do that.'

'What about ghosts then?'

'Have you ever seen one?'

'I don't know.'

'I certainly haven't. People only say they've seen ghosts to make little boys and little girls frightened. But they haven't seen ghosts really.'

He remembered the blind bat, the fox and the fairy of the summer before. During his sickness they had flown through the window and pirouetted just in front of him. What had they been? They were surely from the other world?

'I did see a ghost once.'

133

'What did you see?'

'A blind bat, a fox and a fairy.'

'They weren't ghosts. In stories a ghost is always a person.'

'They weren't ghosts then?' This was a new idea which had never occurred to him before.

'No.'

'What were they then?'

'They came from God.'

She swept the hair away from his forehead.

'Your grandfather isn't angry with you. Your grandfather's in heaven. He isn't coming back.'

'Are there any snakes in Ireland?'

'No, there aren't any.'

'Not anywhere? Not even somewhere no one has been?'

'Saint Patrick banished them all. Every single one. You've nothing to fear.'

He closed his eyes.

'Will you sleep now?' she asked.

'Can you leave the light on?'

'I'll leave it on in the hall. Shall I take Didi out?'

He shook his head.

Mrs McKenna bent forward. He felt her lips on his cheek and smelt the cold, lanoline smell of her face cream.

'Sleep now.'

She slid away across the room.

'Lie down, Didi, lie down,' he heard her saying. 'Good dog.'

The light went out. Mrs McKenna creaked up the stairs. The dog respiring in the darkness was strangely comforting and he knew that he would sleep. He could foretell the pattern precisely. He would sleep lightly at first and then, when the first light began to glimmer beyond the window and the birds began to murmur outside, he would fall into a deep and dreamless slumber. His secret was safe and, for the time being anyway, it seemed that grandfather was well and truly gone.

Chapter Eight

The light inside the church had a blue tinge to it on account of where the ceiling was painted blue between the rafters. The colouring always gave him the feeling of being underwater.

He discreetly surveyed his relatives, stiff in their mourning clothes beside him; granny, uncles James and Thomas; their wives, aunties May and Pat; and his auntie Bridget at the end. He had been hoping that Philomena would come, but she was too young, everyone had said, for such a sad occasion. For him it was his second funeral, so different from the first, and he was able to look about with a certain detachment. Around the eyes of everyone lined up beside him he saw there was a glaze of tears trapped there by the wrinkles. Father Murphy's rapid Latin echoed around the walls. Behind his bare knees he could feel the always damp, always sticky wooden pew.

His granny turned her head and looked down at him. She was wearing a black hat held in place with a black-ended pin and a piece of black veiling hung over her face. Her eyes were grey and wet. She took out a small sodden hankerchief from the sleeve of her jacket and wiped her nose, red and chafed from having been wiped so many times before. Then she nodded her head in the way she always did when she thought manners were slipping and he turned his attention to the front again.

Father Murphy was tall in white and purple. His nose was purple too, swollen and fascinating like an obscure vegetable. The coffin lay behind on rough trestles. The wood was the dark colour of whiskey and the handles were shining brass. Once they got it into the ground and buried, grandfather would be gone for ever, his secret about the fire would be safe and he and granny would go an live in old Andy's cottage together, now that old Andy had gone to the hospital where he would stay until he died. Wicked as it was, he knew, to think it, it was a glorious future that was going to begin once the last spadeful of earth went on. He looked up and saw the pale, pained face of Jesus looking down, the mysterious initials INRI on the scroll at his feet. Granny had once told him that Jesus could read the thoughts of any man if he choose to do so. But as there were so many men's thoughts to be read in the world, he hoped his own would be passed over.

When they came out of the church he found the day grey and slightly chilly. Leaves were burning in the garden of the Creamery Manager's house directly opposite, blue smoke curling upwards from behind a hedge of yew. Mr Mullins the undertaker had left the lights of the hearse on during the service and the battery was flat. He bent down with his uncles and grasped the fender, ready to push and pleased to be seen doing something grown up. The metal was wet for some reason although it had not been raining.

'What an eejit!' whispered uncle James. 'Leaving the lights on!'

Behind the black window of the hearse, filthy and spattered with a thin scum the colour of vinegar, lay the coffin, beautified with flowers and wreaths.

'This must weigh a ton!' muttered uncle Thomas.

They began to push. The tyres crunched on the tarmac and little bits of wet grass fell off the hub caps. All down his back legs his sinews hardened under the skin like elastic stretched until it goes solid. In the rear view mirror he saw reflected Mr Mullins' bovine eyes, whilst a large St Christopher attached by thread danced underneath.

They puffed to the top of the small hill outside the church and gave a final push to get the vehicle over the hump. His uncles straightened up wearily and touched their lower backs. Paul wiped his hands on his trousers.

'I'll give that Mullins flat batteries!' said uncle James.

The mourners began their slow descent behind the coasting hearse towards the graveyard at the bottom. On either side the village lay silent except for rooks calling in faraway trees. Heels scuffed; a handbag clicked open and shut; close by, someone loudly blew their nose. He glanced back and saw that it was Joseph. He was holding a big, grubby hankerchief to his face and wearing his new spectacles with black plastic rims. They had already broken and were mended in the middle with yellowing sellotape.

At the bottom Mullins pulled on the handbrake with a squeak. Everyone crowded up and stood about in silence.

Mullins climbed out and undid the dirty bit of cord which held the back shut. Uncle James rolled his eyes and exclaimed. The door creaked back. His uncles bent forward, removed the wreaths that had adorned the coffin and handed them around. Paul was given a plastic dome. It was so filled with condensation that the flowers inside were only a blur of colour, reminding him of what it was like to look through a broken kaleidoscope. The coffin slid forwards. Before the funeral there had been some talk of his being a pall-bearer, which, to his immense relief, had been abandoned in the end because of his size. As the coffin was lifted up and then lowered onto four dark shoulders he felt a certain sense of relief. Now there was no chance whatsoever that he might be asked to step forward.

The pall-bearers wobbled through the graveyard gateway like an ungainly caterpiller. The mourners filed afterwards. Beechnuts were strewn on the ground, sodden and springy like sponges underfoot. The church bell tolled mournfully in the distance. The first gravestone was a marble anchor, dark moss in the cracks, commemorating a sailor killed in the war. The sailor's family, he knew, were Protestants. It was a mixed graveyard. Their grave was in the farthest corner, a dark hole like a missing tooth.

The coffin went on the ground opposite the pile of earth taken out to make the grave. The soil was mainly black with some yellow clay and with many stones in it. The idea that clean wood was soon to be dirtied he found distasteful. Everyone gathered round and stood uncomfortably in their best shoes on the uneven grass.

There was more speaking. Some in Latin, mostly in English. The wafer thin pages of Father Murphy's prayer book rustled in the wind. Animal noises sounded distantly. Joseph on the other side of the grave, sniffled and looked sad. The coffin was lowered on ropes. His uncles' knuckles went white and their faces went red. The casket settled. The ropes were pulled away.

Earth clattered on wood, a mournful hollow sound that said 'death' to him more than anything so far. A nod from granny and he threw on a handful of his own. There was a quiet whisper of prayer. Father Murphy nodded and a green piece of imitation lawn was drawn over the hole. The service was ended.

Some people came up and shook his grubby hand. Condolences were whispered. There was mud clogged to his shoes. He went to the corner and discreetly began to scrape it away with a stick. The air smelt of Woodbines. Nearby the two gravediggers smoked and spoke discreetly.

'Did you hear the news?' asked one.

'What?'

'There's nothing in that coffin that just went down, only a handful of cinders.'

'Sshh!'

Paul's face went red. Did they suspect his eavesdropping? A hand caressed his shoulder.

'Your grandmother is waiting for you. I shall accompany you both to the hotel.'

He followed Father Murphy back along the path, scuffing his shoes on the kerb to complete the process of cleaning. Black figures floated in the distance. The green covering was off and the grave-diggers were spading in the earth.

'Two funerals on Saturday.'

'No peace for the wicked. . . .'

In the sky above, he noted with something like satisfaction, there was a cloud shaped like a winged snake which appeared to be floating away.

Chapter Nine

Andy's cottage had a stable door at the front. Paul pulled open the top half and saw the young postman outside. He was sitting astride his bicycle, balancing with one hand against the wall.

'Something special for you today,' he said.

He took a letter from the canvas bag hanging around his neck and handed it across. The address was typewritten and there was an English stamp in the corner. Paul's heart began to thump.

'Where's your grandmother?' he asked.

'Out the back.'

Paul turned the letter over casually and registered first the neat, square handwriting with which he was so familiar, and then what was written there:

O. Weismann,
139, Vivian Lane,
Wembley,
London,
England.

It was his father writing from the London house.

'Now you be sure to go and give it to her straight away,' said the postman, and with that he began to pedal away, his chain clattering like a tin-can tied behind a newly marrieds' car.

Paul ran out and found granny at the end of the garden on a little stepladder. She was picking yellow apples with wrinkled skins and putting them in a wooden crate.

'A letter for me!' she said, dismounting the steps and wiping her hands on her apron.

Paul handed it across.

'Go inside,' she said.

He looked at her without moving.

'Go inside!' she repeated.

He turned and began to pick his way sullenly along the flat stones of the garden path. Behind him he could hear her tearing open the envelope.

When he reached the back door he stopped by the rain barrel. Drip, drip, drip, went the pipe that reached down from the gutter.

'Paul! This is the last time I'm telling you. . . .'

He went into the kitchen and sat down at the table. What could he do? He took the sugar bowl and began to spoon through the sugar, searching for the brown lumps which mysteriously grew there. Every time he found one he laid it on the table.

'Paul,' his granny called. Her voice had something in it implying the worst.

He left eight brown lumps arranged in a circle and ran through the door. At the bottom of the garden granny was back on the ladder. Halting behind, he noticed her varicose veins like blue wormcasts and swellings on her legs like lumps in a cheap mattress.

'I have something to tell you,' she said without turning round to face him. 'You'll be going back to England soon. Your father will be coming to collect you. He wrote to me in the letter that just came.'

'Will I be coming back?'

'I'm sure you'll come back for your holidays.'

'I won't be living here then?'

'No,' she whispered.

'But I don't want to go away from you. I'm starting school.'

She plucked an apple and put it in the box. A sour smell drifted up from the rotting ones in the grass.

'Will I have to go to school in England?'

'All children have to go to school. It's the law.'

'But I don't like the school there and you said I could go to school here!'

'I know love, I know I said that. If you were staying with me, you would go to school here. But you can't stay here. You're going back to England.'

'I don't want to go back.'

'It's the will of God.'

'I won't.'

'You have to.'

'I don't want to live with my father.'

'Now Paul. . . .'

'I don't like my father.'

'You mustn't say such things or think such things ever again. I'm ashamed of you. It's a sin to think or say those things.'

'But granny, you said you were my mother now.'

Her legs started to shake. He looked up and saw she had put her hands over her eyes.

'Paul, go inside please.'

The skin hanging under her neck began to wobble.

'Won't you ask father if I can stay here with you . . .?'

'Go inside.'

' . . . and I could just go to him at holiday time and at Christmas.'

'Go inside I said.'

She made a sobbing noise at the back of her throat. She was crying, just like the night he had come back with grandfather from the races.

'Go inside. Go and read the annuals Mrs McKenna gave you.'

He turned round and disappeared into the kitchen. At the bottom of the stairs he stopped. His annuals were in the bedroom but he did not want to read them really. He crept behind the back door, moved aside the old wellingtons that were piled there and peered out through the crack at his granny. Her spasms were shaking the steps. Suddenly the box tumbled off and all the apples spilled on the ground.

She looked at them in amazement and then wearily descended. She was still crying. She wiped her eyes on her apron, squatted down and began to pick them up. She gathered them one at a time and threw them into the box carelessly. It was as if everything was painful and tedious to her. When she finished she stood up and her knees cricked. She was gasping like someone half-drowned. Some of her hair was stuck by wet to her face and she pulled it away. She put the crate back on the steps and climbed up again. Suddenly he was filled with shame. He left his spying place and crept away.

A minute later Paul settled on his bed and opened the Beano annual he had been given at his favourite section.

'Eggcitement at the Egg Factory,' he read.

The cartoon below was one enormous picture spread across two pages depicting a visit by the Bash Street Kids to an Egg Factory. He glanced first at the etiolated, moustachioed, bespectacled school-master.

'Isn't the egg factory eggciting, children?' were the words in the bubble that came out of the master's mouth.

'Isn't sir eggbominable!' muttered the schoolboy immediately behind him.

Close by, two other children 'eggsamined' an ostrich egg.

'Eggnificent,' commented one.

'Eggnormous,' replied the other.

Paul looked up. He was not able to concentrate for the small pain he felt deep inside. He lay back on the pillow and closed his eyes. His mind began to drift and odd details came to him concerning the

London house and the months immediately after his mother's death. . . . He remembered the revolting smell of the sheep's hearts which his father had cooked every night at that time for reasons of economy. Eating the hearts had been purgatory to him. They had been tough and gristly and they had always left him feeling nauseous. He remembered the endless games of cribbage they had played on the long summer evenings, their grubby matches moving up and down the home-made board and the wireless droning in the kitchen, tuned to the home service. Lastly, but most strongly of all, he remembered his bedroom during that wretched summer. It had been – it still was – a low ceilinged, dark room at the back of the house with a small bay window. He had spent all his time there, hunched up and looking out. He remembered what he had seen: miserable gardens, the grass worn by children's feet; lines of washing flapping in the breeze; Mr Aintree's compost heap and Mr Aintree throwing on his tea-leaves morning and night; creosote-covered fences and garden huts all leaning sideways; a row of pebble-dash suburban houses identical to their own. The whole summer he had sat there a fine, grey summer rain had needled down, day in and day out, and every quarter of an hour, the grandfather clock which stood on the landing outside his bedroom door had chimed sadly. . . . The sense that he was returning to all this slowly stole over him. His eyes became moist. He felt a swelling inside and a popping and then a hot tear spilled out of each eye and rolled down each cheek.

Paul lay still in bed. On the other side of the sloping-ceilinged attic room, granny was breathing regularly, almost hypnotically, the rise and fall of her respiration like waves on a beach.

In his mind's eye, he pictured the envelope in which the letter from his father had arrived. It danced before his eyes and expanded to the size of a bill-board. He knew it was downstairs in the kitchen dresser. He knew it was there because when he had been lying in bed earlier that evening, he had heard his granny moving anxiously around the kitchen, opening cupboards and then shutting them again, and muttering to herself. He had crept over to the bannister and peered down. Granny had been by the dresser, the left-hand drawer open in front of her. She had taken the letter out of her apron pocket and put it in away with a great deal of rustling. As she had shut the drawer, he had crept back to bed.

He knew where it was and granny was as fast asleep as she would ever be. The question was . . . ? It was no good thinking about it any more! He lifted back the blankets and rolled onto the floor. The linoleum was cold beneath his feet. He stood still for a moment and listened as his mattress expanded to its normal size.

He started to creep forward. There was a bubble in the linoleum somewhere with a floorboard underneath it which creaked. Where was it? He felt ahead with his big toe, zig-zagging it in front of him. Suddenly he felt it, soft and yielding. He stepped around it and reached the top of the stairs. Granny was still breathing quietly.

He had read once, in a book about spying written specially for children, that stairs only creaked in the middle where they were furthest from support. Gripping the bannister tightly, he stepped onto the first tread with his foot jammed against the wainscotting. The wood sighed, an unassuming sound that blended in with all the other noises that whispered in the lodge at night. He moved his other foot down to the next step and shifted his weight onto it. Again the whisper. Nothing more. Confidently, he moved his first foot and, in this way, he went down the stairs, his body lurching from one side to the other with the wide steps that he took.

He reached the bottom and stepped from the wood – polished with wax and relatively warm – onto the floor, hard-stone and cold. He stopped. His heart was beating. He could feel its thud in the darkness. Ton, ton, ton, it went, like a hammer going on and on. . . .

The bottoms of his pyjamas were slipping. He hitched them up, took a length of the elasticated waist-band and folded it in behind itself.

He looked ahead at the dresser. At the top were the shelves where granny displayed her few new plates. They were white with mauve circles around the rims and different kinds of fruit in the middle; plums, peaches and pineapples. Under the shelves there were two drawers and a cupboard for keeping food that fastened with a black peg on a pin.

Holding his pyjamas by the middle, he started to tread towards it, his eyes fixed on the left-hand drawer with its brass handle. The metal half-moon started to dance before his eyes. He blinked and looked up to the shelves. The plates glimmered in the darkness like light at the end of so many tunnels and at last he reached it.

He re-tucked his pyjamas so tightly that he could feel the elastic around his middle, then slipped his fingers under the brass handle and put the palm of his right hand against the drawer. As he pulled the drawer back he pushed at the same time and, by subtly varying these opposing forces, he was able to slide the drawer out silently.

The drawer hung down before him. A ball of twine, two broken candles and a large fork lay at the front in a heap. At the back of the drawer, placed suspiciously one on top of the other, was a Bushmill's Irish Whiskey ash-tray and a Basildon Bond writing pad. This was surely where the letter was? He slid them aside and found the lining paper underneath was ruffled. He took hold of the corner. It was waxed and stiff. He peeled the paper back, making a small scratching noise, and then there it was; there was the envelope lying face down, the letter sticking out from the torn, ragged top.

There was a scuttling sound nearby. He stood still and listened. The noise stopped. A mouse, he thought. Outside, the wind whispered in the elm trees on the other side of the road.

He lifted the envelope out and crept over to the hearth, where a heap of embers still glowed. He squatted down and withdrew the letter. It was airmail paper, slightly bubbly. He balanced the envelope on the edge of the chair at his side and began to open it. The creases were very hard – he assumed they had been made with his father's ivory pen-knife – and the paper crinkled as he folded it back. When it was done he bent forward and inclined the sheet. It was tricky finding precisely the right angle. At last he found it and began to read:

139, Vivian Lane,
WEMBLEY,
Middx.
Sept. 2nd 1963

Dear Lily O'Berne,

The following information concerning my son Paul Weismann has recently come to my attention:

a) A month ago the Red House burnt down and he was fortunate to escape with his life and without injury.

b) As a result of the shock that he suffered as a consequence, he has not been able to eat properly and is now dangerously thin. In addition to this he is suffering from worms.

c) You have now taken him to live in a sub-standard hovel without proper amenities.

My son was placed in your care on the clear understanding that every best endeavour would be made to ensure his welfare and that you would immediately notify me of any change in his

144

circumstances. But you have not followed the letter of our understanding, have you? All my information comes, not from you, but from someone in the village who had the good sense to pass the facts on to me. I therefore write to give you notice that I intend to exercise my parental rights and reclaim my son. I will arrive on the third of next month. In the meantime there is no need to place him in school. I do not want him in the hands of religious zealots. Finally, if you write to me, I will only return your letters unopened and unread. I had enough letters from one member of your family to last me a lifetime without adding yours to the pile.

Otto Weismann

With slow precision Paul folded the letter and put it back sideways in the envelope, exactly as it had been so that it was sticking out of the top.

The house had grown silent whilst he had been reading and now it was as if it were holding its breath. He listened. He could not even hear granny in their attic bedroom. It was like a tomb.

He stood up, glided back to the dresser and replaced the envelope in the same position he had found it in, lying face down in the corner.

As he covered it over with the lining paper, he recalled how, months before, when he had been walking past the mixed graveyard in the rain, he had looked over the wall and seen the gravedigger covering a half-dug grave with a length of filthy hessian to stop it from flooding.

He lifted the Basildon Bond writing paper and the ash-tray into position and shut the drawer, pushing and simultaneously pulling. Noiselessly it slid back into place.

He crossed the room to the bottom of the stairs and began to climb. Just as he had done on his way down, he trod only on the edges and progress was slow and ungainly. It seemed to take an age before he reached his bedside. He crawled back into the familiar hollow and pulled the covers over himself. The sheets were cold. On the other side of the room granny breathed quietly. He rolled into a ball and turned on his side. His feet were freezing. He pressed them together like hands in prayer. I must not cry! he thought. He closed his eyes, screwed himself up tighter and willed himself to go to sleep.

Moments later a picture sprang into his mind of a great, flat landscape. The surface of the gound was slightly silvery like the

145

back of a mirror. The sky was a light grey which stretched without variation to the horizon. Nothing moved, nothing stirred. There was not a breath of wind or a ray of sunlight. Slowly, he felt his unhappiness receeding, like something borne away on the tide of the sea.

A new image formed in his mind. He was walking along a street. He stepped off the kerb, expecting an instant later to put his foot on the tarmacadamed road. But there was nothing there. His leg jolted and he started to tumble and a moment later he was asleep.

Chapter Ten

Sometime towards morning Paul began to dream: his bed was underneath the massive oak that grew in the middle of Black's Field, not far from the rhododendron bushes. All around the grass stretched away from him in smooth folds. He was leaning on the bedhead with his back to the palings and the charred ruins of the Red House.

A bell began to ring. Its chime was sweet and musical. He looked up and saw that it was hanging from one of the thick branches overhead. The clanger hung down from the middle and at the bottom was attached to a sail. The canvas caught the wind and by this means the bell was rung. Dang, Dang, dang . . . it went. The body of the bell was silver with a thick gold band running around the rim. There was strange writing there which he did not understand. It looked to him as if it was an old language.

From the lower end of the field drifted the baaing sound of sheep. He looked down and saw three men driving a flock towards him. As they drew closer he saw the men were wearing striped robes of many colours and were carrying staves. The legs of the sheep were like spindles, their faces were sooty black and their coats were matted and dirty. The whole scene reminded him of the illustrations in his school Bible which showed shepherds and their flocks in the Promised Land.

The flock came within a few feet of the bottom of his bed and for a moment the air was filled with their monotonous cries, the patter of their feet and the rank smell of their bodies and their dung. The shepherds were calling to each other coarsely in a language he did not speak and banging their staves. They passed by and continued down the field. He watched them until they disappeared from sight.

He was alone. The bell was still ringing. He heard a horse galloping. A huge roan appeared from the direction of the ruins of the Red House. It was ridden by a man in black. They thundered past and galloped into the distance. Paul stared after the rider keenly. He was dressed like a highwayman in a black cape and a black three-cornered hat. He was filled with longing. He wanted to

147

gallop away with the mysterious rider and disappear over the crests of the distant hills. . . .

He began to come awake like something floating up from the bottom of the sea. What had he been dreaming? He lay still without opening his eyes. He remembered he was in bed under a tree. A bell was ringing. A horseman had galloped by. Then he remembered it was the day his father was coming to bring him back to England. The pain came at once. He decided to keep his eyes closed for a moment or two longer. Outside it was raining. He heard it drilling on the tiles above, gurgling along the gutter outside and falling on the fields and trees around the house with a reassuring sous-sous sound like a whisper. In bed it was warm and safe. He heard a car approaching, tyres splashing through puddles. Perhaps it was time already. But how could it be? His granny would have woken him. Perhaps they had overslept? The splashing noises were getting closer. He hurriedly pushed back the covers and scrambled to his knees. The casement was covered with condensation. He rubbed a hole in it and looked through. Outside a white Bedford van splashed by. On the side he read the words 'Healey's High Class Purveyors of Meat.' The road was dark with wet; oily; the colour of tar. Their demesne wall on the far side was like sodden wool. A drenched crow splashed into the middle of the road and began to worry something with its yellow beak. In his stomach and at the back of his throat Paul felt a raw feeling. It was hurt and numbness mixed together. It was like a hardening, as if underneath his skin a layer of stone had formed; a shield of it where he felt the pain in the weak part of his stomach and another at the back of his throat. Both shields made it hard to breathe. It was the same as the feeling that had come after his mother had died.

He climbed down on to the cold floor. His underclothes were laid in a neatly ironed pile on the chair. He unbuttoned his pyjama top and pulled on the vest smelling of starch and his granny.

'Are you up?' she asked from below in her sad voice. He knew it well. She had used it when grandfather had come back drunk from the races and later after he had died. He had always heard it as if it came from a distance, unconnected and remote from himself, but that, he realised glumly, was now a fact of the past.

He took off the bottom of his pyjamas and pulled on his underpants. He wanted to pee. There was a bucket under the bed but he knew he would not be able to go with his granny downstairs and perhaps overhearing. Of late it had become harder and harder for him to use it, even under the cover of darkness. He sat down on the

148

bed with his socks and looked at his toes. The night before his granny had cut his toenails along with his fingernails and, when she had finished, she had gathered the pieces up and put them into an envelope along with a lock of his hair. He pulled the socks on, the jagged ends of his nails catching against the wool and giving him a funny feeling at the bottom of his spine. Drops of rain clattered along the roof above his head like a shower of stones. He went over to the wardrobe and pulled down the long trousers from the hanger hooked over the door. Granny had bought them in Limerick for his return to England to replace his short ones. She had not been able to afford a new jacket but the trousers matched them quite well. He put his feet through the trouser legs. The terylene felt itchy on his skin. He zipped them up and fastened his belt. It really was his last morning. Granny was waiting downstairs. She was sad. She had been sad for weeks. He picked up his things and padded in his stockinged feet towards the stairs.

When he got down to the kitchen he found granny sitting at the table staring out of the window.

'Hullo darling,' she said.

She rose slowly to her feet and sidled towards the stove.

'I'm so stiff today, I feel like a turnip,' she said.

Her steps were short and listless and she kept her face averted. She was not going to look at him, nor was she going to let him look at her.

He laid his clothes over a chair back and went to the bowl on the table. The white enamel was chipped at the edges revealing black iron beneath like rotten teeth in a mouth. Granny carried over the huge kettle and poured in the water. Steam rose in wreaths.

'Let it cool a moment.'

She turned away with the kettle. He tested the water. It was bearable. He peered through the window. The green hedge of honeysuckle was waving frantically in the wind. On the far side of the road the gates to their Avenue banged one against the other. They were fastened together with a knotted piece of chain.

'Bend forward then.'

He put his face right into the water and blew out of his nose. His father had immersed himself like that every morning of his life, only his father had used cold water and had kept his eyes open. He lifted his dripping face and offered it to the flannel slithery with soap. The feeling of her crooked fingers as she washed him brought back the feelings of hurt. He put his head back in the water, came up and blindly found the towel. It smelt of flour because she kept it

149

by the flour bags. Water trickled down his neck. Her fingers rubbed his scalp. He blinked open his eyes as the towel came away. Granny looked at him, her eyes brown and moist.

'Oh my darling.'

She put her arms around him, put her cheek against his and squeezed.

'Will you write to me?'

'Yes I will.'

'How often?'

'Every week.'

'Every week darling.' She squeezed him harder. He felt her cheek-bone pressing against his. On the window ledge the new alarm clock was ticking loudly.

'We mustn't tarry.'

She took the bowl of suddy water and disappeared through the back door. A breeze wafted in full of wet. The turf piled outside was black with the wet instead of its usual brown colour and Lassie and Rover, sodden, were crouched underneath it. He pulled on his shirt, crisp and white, and fastened the black buttons down the front. His father had bought it for his mother's funeral in a large department store in the suburbs of north London. The pipe in the wall started to thump as granny ran the outside tap to rinse the bowl. He separated the brown comb from the hairbrush and began to pull it through his hair. Tangles everywhere, same as every morning. Why was his hair so inclined to tangle? It was the one respect in which he took after his grandfather.

Granny returned and shut the door.

'Egg for breakfast?'

There was nothing he wanted less than to eat and there was nothing he knew that would offend her more than to refuse.

'Two?'

'Two. Yes granny.'

'Am I your dearest granny?' She stood beside him and touched his face.

'You're my dearest thing. Nothing is dearer to me in the world than you. You were my second chance, darling.'

'I'll be back for holidays.'

'Of course you will.'

'When will I be back?'

'That depends on your father.'

'I'll save up for it.'

'I'll send the fare.'

150

She smoothed the top of his head and sighed quietly. He smiled at her and she moved her jaw back at him in imitation of a smile.

'This isn't going to boil potatoes.'

She went over to the stove and put on a pan to boil. He sat down and reached under the table for his newly polished shoes.

'How long does it take to get to England?'

'From here to Dublin, that's a long way. From Dublin to Wales on the other side of the sea, that must be....'

As he pulled on his shoes his finger-ends were smeared from the residue of polish that was on them.'

'... I couldn't tell you how far it is.'

'But it's not as far as America?'

'No.'

'How long did it take you when you went to America?'

'Oh, it was all so long ago I don't remember anymore. I was sea-sick for most of the journey and I lost all sense of time.'

He stood up and put his arms into his jacket, the same one he had worn to both funerals and to the races. It smelt of chemicals. Granny had had it dry-cleaned in town for the journey back. He buttoned it up. Despite the alterations she had made, it was still tight across the shoulders and under the arms.

'I'm just going down the path,' he said, using their euphemism for the privy.

When he stepped outside the wind hit him and where he was still damp behind the ears his skin went terribly cold.

Outside the window that looked onto the road a large shape appeared and stopped. The lazy, familiar noise of the engine drifted in for a moment or two and then cut off.

'It's your father. Go out to him.'

His collar felt uncomfortable around his neck. He got to his feet.

'Offer him some tea.'

His fingers found the latch with matted greasy string wrapped around the end. His polished shoes creaked on the wet path. Drops of water cascaded from the garden gate as he swung it back. The Riley was long, sleek and green. Through the side-windows he glimpsed his father in his thick rimless spectacles with lenses that were faintly mauve. He was holding his scarf down with his chin as he arranged it over his chest. Paul knew the mannerism well. Every time they had ever prepared for a walk, his father had always held his scarf down in this way and arranged it fastidiously. He skirted around the silver fender and curving boot. The driver's door opened and his father climbed out, pulling on a flat cap.

He nodded curtly. 'Hullo Paul,' he said.

'Hu...llo father.'

His father towered above him, his big mouth glinting with gold fillings.

'Did you have a good trip?'

'You sound like a debutante.'

Paul's face went red.

'Granny wondered....' He swallowed and hoped he would not stammer.

'Granny wondered if you might like a cup of tea?'

He had forgotten how frightened his father made him feel. This new sensation mingled with the hurt.

'No thank you. Let's get this business over and done with. I want to catch the evening boat. Are your bags packed?'

'Yes.'

'Go and get them then.'

His father turned a key and lifted the boot. A little light came on inside. Paul went down the path. A fine rain had fallen on his face. He wiped his cuff across his forehead. Lassie appeared around the corner, her fur like sodden brown carpet. He gave her a peremptory stroke and went inside.

'Granny?'

The kitchen was empty. He wiped the dog's wet away on the side of his jacket. The back door was open and from beyond came an ugly sound.

'Granny.'

He went through the back door and found her bent over the drain by the outside tap. A small spear of vomit lengthened from her mouth like nougat. She looked up at him. Her eyes were dark. She retched and the end of the spear dropped towards the drain. 'Go away!' she hissed gesturing with her hands. 'Go away.'

He went back into the kitchen and banged the door. At the back of his thoat he could taste his own bile rising – the bitterest of tastes. Through the wall the retching sound came faintly. He went and stood in the middle of the kitchen. His father was beyond the honeysuckle outside the window, hat off, smoothing back his luxuriant black hair and staring down the road. Paul picked up his brown suitcase from the bottom of the stairs and lugged it to the door. Outside the label attached to the handle fluttered in the wind,

152

reminding him of holding a butterfly cupped between his palms. His father took the suitcase at the gate. He ran back. Inside the kitchen granny was waiting with a pale face for him, a cardboard box on the table beside her.

'Here darling,' she said.

She slipped an envelope and a small square packet into his pocket.

'There's something from me and a pound from Mrs McKenna and ten shillings from Joseph, God bless him. Will you write and thank them?'

He nodded.

'Get your coat.'

His fingers found the money envelope and then the packet. There was something in the packet that was hard but he could not tell what it was. He took his fawn duffle coat off the hook and pulled it on.

'Does he want any tea?'

'I don't think so.'

She picked up a cardboard box and they stepped outside and went down the path. The wind was roaring, sending clouds skeetering across the sky. At the gate a squall of rain hit their faces causing them to blink. The adults nodded a greeting at one another.

'Would you like some tea or some refreshments before continuing your journey?' granny asked politely.

'No I won't. I want to get to Dun Laoghaire by six.'

She handed Paul the cardboard box. It was packed with six jars of jam and a cake of his favourite bread wrapped in a tea towel. He put them down beside the suitcase and his father closed the boot.

'Well, goodbye and thank you very much for looking after Paul.'

His father extended a hand and his granny shook it.

'He was only pleasure,' she said, 'and never any trouble.'

His granny bent towards him and folded her arms over his shoulders. She kissed him on the cheeks. Out of the corner of his eye he noticed his father disappearing round the side of the car.

'Goodbye,' he said.

'Goodbye my darling.' She squeezed and squeezed.

'I don't want to go.'

'I know that.'

'When I grow up I'll come back.'

The car engine coughed into life.

'You'd better go.'

She gave him a last squeeze and released him. He opened the door. Inside the car his father was adjusting the rear-view mirror.

'Get in the back,' his father said quietly, 'and careful of the paintwork on the sill.'

Careful of the paintwork on the sill! How often had he heard that order before. On every shopping trip, on every outing, on every holiday.

He tipped the front passenger seat forward and took a giant step into the cavernous, carpeted rear. It smelt of old leather and the wax which his father rubbed in to prevent the upholstery from cracking. The front passenger seat was brought forward and clicked down. His granny shut the door. His father turned on the engine and the indicator came on. They began to glide forward. His granny's face slid past. She put her hand against the glass, her wedding ring sounding like a pebble thrown against it. Her palm was creased with lines. He saw every one of them and he knew he would never forget them. They drove on. He turned and saw her bent figure through the curved back window. Her arm was raised, waving. He waved back. Smaller and smaller she became and then they lurched around a corner and she disappeared behind a hedgerow. He turned and faced forward again.

'Have a good cry if you want,' he heard his father saying. 'Here's a hanky.'

He took the starched, folded hankerchief and stared out of the window. Outside he saw ragged hedgerows, crumbling gateways and fields so sodden their green had turned to grey. A long time passed and then he remembered the packet in his pocket. He took it out and ripped it open. Inside he found two green pound notes from his granny and a set of rosary beads.

'What are you doing?'

'It's a present granny gave me.'

'What is it?'

'Rosary beads.'

'Have you been going to Mass?'

'No.'

'Wind down the window.'

He bent over the front passenger seat and began to turn the handle.

'Right down.'

Borne in with the cold, wet air came the sound of their tyres splashing in the pools of water by the roadside.

'Now throw them away.'

He formed the beads into a tight ball and threw them into the hedgerow. Then he wound up the window and sank back in his seat. The front windscreen misted up and his father turned on the de-mister. The air came out with a whine and the condensation began to recede. He wondered if he was going to cry. It would be nice to cry, he thought. It would be a relief. He imagined the hot salty taste of his tears, his eyes burning, the sensation of hardness in his solar plexus and at the back of his throat slowly dissolving. He opened his mouth and forced the pressing feeling inside that infallibly brought them on. But rather than tears flowing and bringing with them a sense of release, the feeling of hardness only increased. It gradually spread under his skin until he felt his whole body was completely encased in it, as if he were wearing a suit of armour. He put his cheek against the cold side-window and looked out, for what he imagined would be the last time, at the cold, sodden landscape flashing by.

Epilogue

He pulled up in front of McKenna's. The Austin Cambridge which
had taken him on so many excursions was gone, replaced with a
children's climbing frame. The old was giving way to the new. It
was the same story everywhere. The Creamery Manager's house
had become a car park. The post office had become a Spars
supermarket. Finch's bar had become 'The Lord Sarsfield', all
pebble-dash and brown guttering with a blackboard outside which
announced 'Pub Grub Here'.

He slipped the clutch. The car rolled forward. Fifty yards down
the road a stained wooden sign gave the name of the first new
bungalow as 'Glendalough'. The brand new building with a cart-
wheel by the door stood in a quarter of an acre of mud, surrounded
by abandoned building materials and beer barrels sawn in half in
which a few scrawny geraniums were struggling to survive. An old
woman stood behind net curtains and watched him as he passed.
The original homestead stood behind, fallen thatch green with
slime.

The road wound on. A new garage, Corkrin's, bright new trac-
tors outside like toys. More new dwellings. Then suddenly the road
bent to the right – it was much less dramatic than he remembered it
– and there they were: the gates leading to their avenue on one side
and old Andy's cottage, the lodge, on the other.

He drove over to the cottage. Over the years the honeysuckle
had grown wild. Its sweet scent hung in the air. He pushed open the
gate and went down the weed-covered path. A bright new padlock
hung from the door. He bent towards the window. Inside it was
dark and all that he could see was the kitchen table, a basin resting
on top with a child's doll inside: naked with unreal pink-coloured
flesh, one eye open, one eye shut, long synthetic eyelashes. Of
course! it was Philomena's. . . .

Two years after his father had brought him back to London, he
had received granny's second Christmas card. Inside he had found a
two-pound postal order and the inscription 'To dearest Paul with
love from his granny and Philomena'. He had been supplanted. She
had taken his cousin to live with her as elderly people in the district

156

often did when there were relatives with large families to draw on. He had wept bitterly, but by the following July, when his next birthday came round, a repeat of the inscription no longer had the same effect. Over the months he had become reconciled to the idea. Every Christmas and birthday thereafter, cards had faithfully come, and always signed by granny on her and Philomena's behalf in her funny sloping writing and always containing a postal order for the same sum.

In his twenty-first year a letter addressed to him in handwriting he did not recognise had found him out at university. It came from Philomena and it told him his grandmother had died in a Dublin hospital after a short illness. Shortly afterwards came a second describing the funeral with a copy of the Will enclosed. Only the Lodge, the lawn and the yard buildings were left, the rest of the fields having been sold off over the years to support the two of them. Philomena had been left all that remained and as soon as she was sold up she informed him she was leaving Ireland. The night of the second letter, mingled feelings of annoyance at his grandmother, for not having left him the share that he felt was his by right, and regret for his own laxity had overwhelmed him. He had gone to bed early. But by the following morning the mood had passed, and after that he had not thought much about his eleventh summer at all.

He drove across the road and climbed out. The gates still hung at their slightly odd angle. Tongues of rust snaked down the piers below the hasps. Behind, the avenue stretched through a sea of yellow ragwort and purple thistles towards the ruins of the Red House. He swung the gates back grating on their hinges. The clouds parted and sun filtered down.

Driving up the pock-marked avenue, the car rose and fell like a boat at sea. The bitter smell of ragwort drifted through the open window and he tasted it like metal at the back of his throat. The low hanging branch of an ash tree slapped like spray against the windscreen. He ducked and blinked involuntarily. The once-green corrugated chicken runs loomed up beside him like an outcrop of rock. Tyres cut in half leant against the sides. Twice daily, when these had been troughs, granny had filled them with sour milk and yellow meal while her chickens clamoured around her. The avenue swung away to the left and he followed it around to the point where it petered out at the side. He turned off the ignition and climbed out.

Wind stirred the copper beeches. It was a dry noise and more suggestive of that place than any other. The ornamental gates were gone, replaced with a length of red plastic. He climbed over and walked towards what had been the front door. On either side the stone pineapples peeped through a riot of brambles and greenery, like sacred artefacts in a jungle. He stopped before the front steps of granite. Over the years the earth had moved, both throwing them up and breaking them in two. He sniffed the air. It smelt sweet and sickly. Cow parsley grew all over the ruins in rich profusion. He started walking again. The overgrown remains of the parlour sprawled beside him. He lifted his eyes. A hundred yards away the grey stone walls of the yard showed above the unruly evergreen hedge. The oak felled by lightning lay between and, closer to hand, he noticed a bulldozer and dumper truck.

He passed the remains of the kitchen and emerged onto the flag. Crab apple trees with their lichen-covered branches the colour of corroded copper crouched at the back, and in the furthest corner stood the Pumping Hut leaning at a dangerous angle. Some way down the lawn there was a figure heading towards him. He strode over to the latch gate and observed the person's progress. It was a man in wellingtons and a coat. The man swung his stick at a thistle and sent up a cloud of seed-down. There was something familiar about his gait. The man drew closer and acknowledged Paul with a wave.

'Hullo,' greeted Paul.

'Hullo,' replied the man.

As soon as he heard the voice he realised who it was. It was Joseph. He waited. Joseph came up to the latch gate, lifting the loop of wire holding it shut, and stepped through.

'Hullo Joseph! Don't you remember me?'

They looked at each other. Joseph still wore spectacles and his skin was still like an uncooked sausage.

'Do I know you?' Joseph asked. 'Are you from the Pools?'

'Don't you remember me? I'm Paul.'

After thinking for a while longer Joseph started to smile. 'I remember you. You're Paul. Of course I remember you. You were this high. . . .'

Joseph indicated a young boy.

' . . . So you've come back to see us?'

'Yes.'

'Not the same place at all, is it?'

'No.'

'It's a far cry from your day. Look over there! Look at that factory!'

158

Joseph pointed at three huge chimneys on the far side of the river, grey smoke curling out of them.

'Oh yes, there've been a lot of changes. We've got skinheads now you know!'

'What's happening here, Joseph?'

'Oh, there's big changes around here now. You wouldn't recognise the place.'

'Are they building here on the Red House?'

'They are. The manager's house they're building here.'

'The factory manager?'

'Yes, the factory manager. He's a German. He's a very decent man. They're building him a house here. His wife is coming from Germany. And his family.'

'The factory own the land?'

'The factory own the land. They bought it all.'

'From Philomena?'

'They did. Mrs O'Berne your grandmother died, may the Lord have mercy on her soul, and Philomena sold the land to the factory. They paid a very good price, I hear.'

There was a pause and then Joseph asked abruptly, 'Do you live in England?'

'Yes I do.'

'Philomena is in England.'

'Is she?'

'Do you ever see Philomena?'

'Well I haven't run into her. England's a very big place you know.'

'Oh I know that. She sold the land, and she went to Southampton, I heard.'

'That's on the south coast. It's a very big town.'

'She's a hairdresser now. She has a place there.'

'She must be doing very well.'

'She went several years ago. She hasn't been back.'

'She hasn't been back to visit?'

'No.'

'She must like it there!'

'She must. Do you live in London?'

'Yes.'

'My younger brother is in London.'

'Oh yes. Where does he live in London?'

'He lives in Willesden. Do you know Willesden?'

'Not really.'

159

'Yes, he lives in Willesden. That's where he lives.'

'And what are you doing now, Joseph?'

'Oh nothing much. Just you know, labouring and that. I work for the factory. They still have a few cattle on the land roundabouts. I water them and fodder them and keep an eye on them, you know.'

Joseph gestured towards the corrugated hut where the water pump was housed. On the walls were scorch marks dating from the fire, like a bruise under the skin.

'I've come up to turn on the pump and fill up the old trough. The beasts'll be up presently.'

The trough, quarter-full, glimmered in the field behind him.

'Do the factory pay a good wage?'

'Oh I couldn't say. . . .'

Joseph smiled, revealing a gap where his two front teeth should have been.

' . . . I'm married now, you know. I have six children.'

'That's a large family.'

'Six children, yes, that's a large family. Are you married yourself?'

'No.'

'You're not.'

'Not yet.'

'Well, I have to get on now and get home to my dinner. If I don't buck up it'll get cold.'

Joseph disappeared inside the corrugated hut and the coughing sound of the electric pump started up. Paul stared over the hedge at the water-trough. The rim gleamed like silver. It had been buffed that way over the years by the slack jaws of drinking cattle. The pipe at the side went into spasms and water started to gush out of the end with a metallic hiss.

Joseph came out of the hut.

'I'll be going now,' he said.

'Well goodbye, it's been nice talking to you.'

Paul held out his hand and Joseph took it shyly. His grasp was extremely limp.

'Bye-bye,' he said like a child.

Joseph left through the latch gate and set off down the field. He walked smartly and did not once look back. Paul watched him until he disappeared under the dark oaks. Joseph was taking the short cut to the road.

A huge cloud hung in the sky looking like a bag of soot about to explode. The factory siren sounded distantly across the fields. He

160

imagined the afternoon shift streaming through the factory gates. In half an hour they would be scattered in bungalows across the parish, sitting in kitchens smelling slightly of gas, eating fry-ups under humming fluorescent strips and listening to the sports round-up on the radio. . . .

On the far side of the hedge the black heads of the approaching bullocks glided by like targets in a shooting gallery. A moment later came the slurping sound as their furry tongues lapped the water.

I wonder, he thought to himself.

He turned around and followed the hedge along for a few feet until he was level with the door of the pumping hut. That was more or less the spot, he estimated.

He squatted down and parted the side of the hedge. Inside everything was dark and confused. His sight began to adjust and he noticed six or seven boughs all radiating from the same root. If he was not mistaken there was a hollow in the middle of them.

Turning his head sideways he thrust his arm in. The coarse, green leaves as they brushed his cheeks were cold. He found a crack between two boughs and inserted his hand. He had been right. There was a hollow in the middle.

He began to burrow through the vegetable detritus that had gathered there over the years. Close to the bottom his fingers found something cold and glassy. In a few moments, he would know if it was what he was looking for.

He wriggled his hand underneath the object and began to lift upward. The dense inner growth resisted his progress and twice sharp ends tore across the back of his knuckles. With a final wrench he pulled his hand free and saw that he was holding a jam jar. It was streaked with mud and packed with debris, and in the very bottom, combined into a solid lump by the forces of wet and time, were his lost pennies.

He woke up and found himself in a large double bed. The woollen curtains over the windows were lit up by the sun outside. He turned on the radio and swung out of bed. A jig crackled out of the loudspeaker. On the bedside table lay the Gideon Bible which he had been reading the night before, and the blank laundry list stamped with the name of the motel which he had used as his book marker sticking out of the top.

He rose to his feet and padded to the window. The curtains

161

swished back and he blinked in the sun. Green fields stretched away from him towards the grey, crenellated shape of Dromoland Castle.

He went into the bathroom and turned on the light. A fan came on and began to whine. His long lost jam jar stood by his wash-bag. He ran the cold water tap. His unhappiness deriving from the past was a lump as solid as the corroded money. But with care it could be taken apart and, like the pennies, polished up into something else. He would buy notebooks, he decided. They would be ruled with feint margins. He would write everything down. He dropped his head under the tap and ran the cold water through his hair.